PRINCESS OF ATHELIA

AYA LING

PRINCESS OF ATHELIA

INTRODUCTION

Kat has now moved into the palace, determined to make the most of her time with her beloved prince. Being princess, however, is no bed of roses. She must learn how to behave like a royal, prepare for the upcoming engagement, and defend herself against hostile relatives. And knowing that her time with Edward is limited, Kat isn't so certain that she wants to be princess anymore...

This is a companion novella (Book 1.5). Reading order should be like this:

The Ugly Stepsister (Book 1)
Princess of Athelia (Book 1.5)
Twice Upon a Time (Book 2)
Ever After (Book 3)
Queen of Athelia (Book 4)

"I simply fail to comprehend what Edward sees in you."

I try to make my smile appear as sincere as I can manage. Lady Petunia, aka Her Most Honorable Duchess of Somerset, has called upon me for afternoon tea, and there's no way I can refuse. We sit in a small pavilion in the palace gardens, sipping sweetened ice tea, while a gentle breeze wafts in the air. It should be peaceful, it should be delightful, but the atmosphere couldn't be more unbearable.

She's Edward's aunt, I tell myself. *And Henry's mother. And Elle's future mother-in-law. So don't antagonize her, no matter how much you feel like pelting her with macaroons.*

"Perhaps you can ask him," I offer in the sweetest tone I can muster.

"Those freckles!" The duchess holds up a monocle and peers closely at me as though I'm some insect under a microscope. "Really, child, have you not tried anything to remove those freckles? It is imperative that you look flawless on your wedding day."

A pang briefly hits me. *Wedding day*. That will also be the day that I leave Edward. Although both of us have agreed NOT to talk about my departure, and I've told myself NOT to think of the inevitable, there are times when I can't help wondering what it will be like when I'm gone. Will I disappear altogether? What about the old Katriona? Krev is missing these days, so I can't ask him about it, and honestly speaking, part of me doesn't even want to because I dread how he'll answer.

"Of course," I say lightly. "The idea of marrying with a freckled nose is simply unpardonable. I forgot there is a written rule that forbids the bride to be anything but absolutely perfect."

She glares at me. "Your attitude could use some pruning, young lady. I need hardly remind you that flippancy is highly unattractive for a girl of your age."

And yet this is why Edward fell in love with me, I am tempted to retort. I look down at my hands, itching to take out my pocket watch. Such a pity that they don't have wrist watches in Athelia.

"I ought to have a word with Madame Dubois," the duchess continues, still frowning. "Now that you are marrying into the royal family, you must learn to conduct yourself with propriety. Tell me, Katriona, is it true that you offered to stand witness for Poppy Montgomery when she ran away to Ruby Red with a solicitor?"

Her words drip with contempt. Having considerable experience with such a condescending tone—thank you, Lady Bradshaw—I just nod and smile as though she's asking what I had for breakfast.

"Good heavens!" The duchess spills tea from her cup. I grab a napkin and hand it to her. "So it *is* true that you supported a thoughtless, headstrong girl's decision to be married without the blessing of her parents?"

"She does have her parents' blessings. Mr. Davenport convinced her father that he is worthy of her, and they had a proper wedding at Sir Montgomery's house."

"She ought to have gained permission first," the duchess says with a sniff. "Such willful disobedience! I am sure, Katriona Bradshaw, that now you are to become a member of the royal family, you will *not* engage in nor encourage such scandalous behavior."

It takes every ounce of restraint not to give her the finger. Luckily, I'm saved from the temptation when my personal maid, Amelie, appears. She's quite attractive, with her hazel eyes, curved cheekbones, and pointed chin. However, she looks even prettier when she smiles, for it brings a sweetness to her usually stern, no-nonsense expression. It's a pity that her smiles are hard to come by.

"A message for Her Highness."

"Is Edward finished with his business?" Usually in the mornings, he has to stay in his room, drafting memorandums, writing letters to foreign ambassadors, and reviewing pages and pages of documents that are akin to law school material and make me squint and yawn. I never knew a prince could be this busy.

"Madame Dubois wishes to see you."

I try hard not to show my displeasure. More lessons on deportment and etiquette, yay. Just when I thought I'd had enough of lady lessons, I have princess lessons. I need to learn how to receive foreign guests, memorize the royal family's history, and even learn how to pair different foods with wine. It's intriguing in the beginning, but when the lessons go from early morning until evening, added to the pressure to flawlessly perform all that royal stuff, the novelty wears off quickly. The life of a royal isn't the way the fairytales paint it—at least, not in Athelia.

"Then she ought not to be kept waiting," the duchess says. "I hope that by the time you are engaged, you will have sufficiently improved."

Seriously, with a mother who is worse than Lady Bradshaw, I wonder how Henry stayed a good kid. I rise and sink into a curtsy. No wobbling at all—I told Amelie I'd need to wear comfortable shoes or she'd be seeing bruises on my knees every day.

"I thank you for your company, Lady Catherine—um, Lady Petunia," I say. *Whoops.* But I've never seen anyone more similar to Lady Catherine de Bourgh than the duchess.

❧

WHEN WE REACH THE END OF THE CORRIDOR, AMELIE TAKES a turn and goes down a flight of winding stairs. I'm still unfamiliar with the palace, but I do realize that we aren't heading to the torture chamber—I mean, the schoolroom—where I have princess lessons.

"Amelie, is Madame Dubois really expecting me?"

"Of course she is," Amelie says.

"Excuse me if I'm wrong, but I don't really think we're heading in the right direction."

"Oh." Amelie doesn't even look back. "His Highness has ordered to have your lessons scheduled for an hour later."

I knew it. Sure enough, when we reach the foot of the staircase, Bertram is there, grinning like a big puppy. He must be happy to see me . . . not. It's Amelie. I have a sneaking suspicion that Edward arranged for Amelie to be my lady-in-waiting because Bertram has a crush on her. Which is not to say that Amelie isn't competent. She's brisk, efficient and loyal, and unlike some of the older, more experienced servants, she never lets me feel like I'm not good enough for Edward. It's just that she's only seventeen but acts like she's thirty—matronly, bossy, and frightfully practical.

"Princess Kat," Bertram exclaims. He briefly glances at Amelie before giving me a magnificent bow. "May I escort you to His Highness's garden?"

"I know the way," I say quickly. "I've been there a dozen times already. Why don't you escort Amelie back to my suite?"

Bertram brightens. Amelie, however, doesn't look too enthusiastic. She crosses her arms and deals me a glance that makes her look just like my kindergarten teacher. "Forgive me, but even with the shortcut it would take about twenty minutes to get from here to His Highness's garden. Since you have lost your way around the palace no less than twice each day, it's far better that Bertram show you the way. You won't be doing him any favors if His Highness has to wait too long to see you."

████—she owns me. I consider arguing that even if I become lost, there will be plenty of other servants to show me the way, but her words have struck a chord.

Bertram strides forward, an urgent look in his eyes. "Allow me take you there right away, Princess Kat."

2

My heart beats faster when I approach that familiar door draped with ivy. No matter how many times I've visited Edward's garden, I still get butterflies in my stomach knowing that he's waiting for me. I take out the big, golden key—he had a duplicate made for me the instant I moved into the palace—and insert it into the keyhole.

No sooner have I closed the door than a hand seizes my wrist and tugs me forward. A blur of royal colors flash in front of me, my chin is lifted, and then warm lips descend on mine— heated, passionate, filled with hunger, like a traveler finally discovering an oasis in the desert. Edward encircles me in his arms, melding my body against his, and I forget everything except trying to stay upright.

I gulp down a huge breath of air when he finally lets me go. "Edward," I chide him. I don't have a mirror with me, but I'm sure my lips are bruised and puffy. I've already endured knowing smirks from Bertram since I moved into the palace. "I have to meet Madame Dubois in an hour. I thought your upbringing had taught you more restraint."

He nuzzles my throat, his hands still resting on my waist. "All morning, I've been chained to my desk. All morning, I've been drafting and reviewing piles of documents. All morning, I've been forced to listen to my subjects drone in a tone that could put an energetic babe to sleep. It is hardly inconceivable that I should crave your presence. Besides,"—he raises his head and stares into my eyes—"I have a matter of utmost importance to discuss."

He looks so serious that I'm tempted to put a finger on either corner of his mouth and tease a grin out of him. But something in his tone makes me drop the notion. And the way he's looking at me—with desperation written in his eyes—it reminds me of that heartbreaking moment when I confessed to him that I wasn't from Athelia.

I place my hands over his. "I'm all ears."

"I heard my parents discussing our wedding date." He swallows and focuses on the ivy-covered wall behind me. "They plan to set it for next June."

That leaves us less than a year. A pang stabs me. Even if the time frame sounds reasonable—long, even—now that we're finally together, next spring seems too soon for us to say farewell.

"Don't we have a say in this? I mean, can't we offer an opinion?"

"Kat, it's traditional for royal weddings to be held in June, for it is named after the goddess of marriage. Besides"—his face reddens—"the schedule is set for the first child to be born the following spring."

I blink. We're not even engaged, and he's already thinking of *children*? Yeah, there's definitely a world's difference between us. I don't want to know what the consequences will be if I return to my family with Edward's child. Maybe it's just as well that there are strict rules for the bride-to-be to remain chaste before marriage. Though, from what I've heard about the many earls and barons, there's no restriction for the groom—another reason I dislike Athelia.

"So . . . unless we can come up with a plausible alternative, the wedding will take place next June?"

"That goblin who is responsible for sending you here . . . was he absolutely certain that you must return when the wedding takes place?"

I nod, feeling tears well up in my eyes. I've asked Krev the same question a million times, until he lost his temper and hasn't shown up since I moved into the palace.

"That's how the spell works. Once the bells start chiming, it'll send me back through a magic portal."

He swallows but gives me a smile that actually seems genuine. "We still have nine months. Let us make them the nine happiest months that I have yet to live."

His words hit the core of my being. I smile back at him but am unable to prevent a tear from sliding down my face.

Edward dabs my cheek with a handkerchief. "*Happy* months, remember?"

"Right." I tell myself to stop being so emotional. Crying will only make both of us feel worse. "Let's make a pact, okay? Don't mention *anything* about my . . . my . . . what's going to happen after the wedding. We're going to be the happiest couple that Athelia has ever seen."

"Which is, actually, a necessity. No one should know that you are not really Katriona Bradshaw. It is imperative that we act like you will stay by my side forever."

It's too much to bear. I wrap my arms around him and cling to him as though that can ease the pain. *Stay with him*, my mind screams. *We've been through this a million times*, another voice in my head answers. *Even if you choose to abandon Mom and Paige, you still can't marry Edward.*

A while later, Edward gently pushes me away. His expression returns to his everyday mask of calm, collected indifference.

"There is another matter I need to mention. Galen returned this morning from his travels."

I distinctly remember that Edward granted Galen a few weeks off to give him a well-deserved break after all that strenuous preparation for the ball. Organizing a nationwide event is no small feat.

"He brought us a letter from Adam Snyder's widow."

Adam Snyder! "He had . . . his wife is still alive?"

"Galen inquired in his circle and tracked her down. I'm not sure how he did it, but during his travels to the earl's manor, he convinced Mrs. Snyder to write a letter of confession. Her written proof will greatly aid us in restoring to Elle her rightful identity and inheritance."

Edward extracts a folded paper and hands it to me. The letter is crudely written, but the message is clear. Mrs. Snyder overheard her husband taking orders from Lady Bradshaw to have Elle drowned. She didn't know that Meg had appeared and forced Adam Snyder to let Elle live, but she did know that the little girl Snyder brought to the capital was actually the earl's daughter. Later, Lady Bradshaw rewarded Adam Snyder with a huge sum of money that paid for his daughter's dowry. Mrs. Snyder even expressed her wish that her husband would be lauded as a hero for saving Elle's life.

I crumple up the letter. I don't know if Mrs. Snyder is being completely truthful, but I don't feel like pursuing the issue any further. It is possible that she believed her husband had defied Lady Bradshaw at the last minute and that she didn't know a fairy had ordered Snyder to preserve Elle's life. Whatever the truth may be, I'm holding proof that Lady Bradshaw tried to have Elle killed—and that Elle is the earl's daughter.

"I'm so glad for Elle," I say. "Although in the beginning, I expected that she'd go from poverty to riches because of you. But this way is even better. She achieved her new status from justice."

"Speaking of justice"—Edward tweaks a lock of my hair—"I have a special gift for you."

I give him a suspicious look. I had long since refused any jewelry or dresses from him as I already have an overflowing wardrobe. Usually he opts to get me books when I can't visit Mr. Wellesley's bookstore, or sometimes he surprises me with flowers from his garden. But as he simply came from a meeting with the Lord Chamberlain, I don't see anything that may indicate a gift.

Edward extracts a card from his pocket. The size isn't much different from that of a calling card, but the card itself is plain white, apart from a red and gold border running along the edge. A paragraph, written by hand, reads: *I hereby grant the Lady Katriona permission to attend the parliament session that will take place on 15 September.* It is signed by the king.

I look up at him. "I . . . don't understand."

"I believe it should be obvious. After all the hard work you have been doing with pushing the eight-hour bill, I thought that you would like to attend the meeting when the Third Reading takes place."

"I'd *love* to see the Third Reading. But are you sure it's okay? Has there been any precedent of a woman in the parliament?"

"The only instances that I can recall are when there is a female monarch on the throne, because it is her responsibility to open the parliament with a formal speech."

Just as I expected. Nevertheless, I'm grateful that he had taken the steps to seek out his father and speak on my behalf.

"Thank you"—I tuck the card securely in my pocket, then rise on tiptoe to kiss his cheek—"for making exceptions for me. Did I tell you again how much I love you?"

He smirks, clearly pleased, and snakes his arm around me again. "What else to expect when I've fallen in love with the most extraordinary girl in the kingdom?"

3

"Name the great-great-great-grandfather of His Highness, Edward."

I don't have a ▓▓ clue. I'm sitting in this gorgeous but stuffy room, where Madame Dubois is making me memorize the royal genealogy—right up to twenty generations back. Guess what? Princess lessons are even more stressful and frustrating and demanding than the lady lessons I had earlier. But I try not to complain; I have to make an effort for Edward's sake. Although the king and queen have assured me that they have no objections to Edward's choice, many people have found it incredible that a plain, insignificant younger daughter of an earl could attract the prince's attention. I don't want to prove them right.

Madame Dubois—a tall, stately woman with huge butterfly-like spectacles—raps her cane on the table. Instead of treating me with more respect now that I'm a princess, she makes me feel like a seven-year-old on her first day of school.

But with genealogy, at least it's only names I have to memorize. Royal protocol is more of a pain ▓▓▓▓▓ with complicated rules that are even more demanding than those for being a lady—like the exact angle I should extend my arm when greeting a subject.

"When you are hostess to forty guests for dinner, what is the precedence of their seats?"

"Um . . ." Can I say that the most guests I've ever had to entertain are . . . five? Last Christmas, we had Grandma and Grandpa over, which made five of us. Then I can't help it—I cover my mouth to stifle a yawn. I'm well aware that it's rude, but being up since six doing nothing but princess lessons is bound to take a toll.

Madame Dubois's eyebrows lift to form a V on her forehead. "You have *hugely* disappointed me, Miss Katriona! I had expected that your mother would have ensured you had a more thorough education." She points a bony finger at a chair placed near the window. "Sit there, and memorize the first ten chapters on the etiquette of royals. I shall be back to test you in an hour. Should you fail to answer any one of my questions, you will be forbidden to go down to lunch. You shall stay here until you have every single rule imprinted in your mind."

I try hard not to appear relieved. Not that the king and queen are that intimidating. But when every meal has three to five courses with an army of servants hovering around and making sure the butter plate is always full and the coffee is always hot, it does get on my nerves. I miss the days when lunch was just Mom, Paige, and me sitting around our tiny kitchen table, making sandwiches and lemonade. I wish I could have that small but homey table here, with just Edward at my side. But privacy in the palace is a luxury.

"Yes, Madame," I say, trying my best to look meek and humbled. I take the heavy book of royal etiquette and sit by the window. It's actually quite nice sitting there, with the late summer air still humid and warm, and hearing the distant chirps of sparrows. If only I could read a Gothic romance instead. And if only I could tuck my feet under my bum and prop a hand against my cheek.

I'm halfway through the book when someone knocks on the door. I fly up with a wild hope that Edward has come to seek me. Maybe the Lord Chamberlain is in a good mood and decided to let him off early.

My heart sinks when Amelie enters. She curtsies and hands me a letter. " 'Tis from Miss Elle, Your Highness. She said it was urgent."

Oh dear. I hope that Lady Catherine de Bourgh—I mean, the duchess—didn't scream at her and declare that she's still unworthy of Henry. At least I have the approval of the king and queen—though that may be due to Edward's reluctance to get married.

"Where's Elle?" I glance at the doorway. "Does she look all right?"

Amelie shrugs. "I invited her to stay for a cup of tea, but she insisted on leaving. Something about seeing a lawyer."

Can it be about her newly acquired inheritance? I tear open the envelope and hastily unfold the letter within.

Dearest Kat,

I have been meaning to visit you as promised, but a recent happening has compelled me to remain indoors for now. A visit to the physician a few days ago has confirmed the happy news: I am with child. Jonathan and Elle have been a constant joy and comfort, yet I do not dare to venture from the house till the symptoms of my pregnancy become more tolerable. I send my regrets but am positive that we shall meet very soon.

Yours truly,

Poppy

I CAN BARELY CONTAIN MY EXCITEMENT. POPPY IS PREGNANT! Needless to say, I can't sit still and continue with my lesson. Too bad she can't come and visit. I had planned to take her on a tour of the royal menagerie. It's the next best thing to the library.

I snap the book shut. Why can't I go and see her instead? She and Elle are the only true friends I've made. Outside the window, I spot Edward heading toward my wing with brisk footsteps. I wave at him, flapping my arms like a windmill, but he doesn't look up.

Frustrated, I do something I haven't done since I was eight: I curve my thumb and forefinger to form a circle and give a shrill whistle. That does the trick. He looks up—along with several courtiers and servants. All of them stare at me as though I'm mad.

Suddenly, I feel like an idiot, but it's too late to undo my action. I may as well make the most of it now that I have Edward's attention.

I curl my forefinger and beckon to Edward like a femme fatale in a movie. "Get here—now," I mouth.

4

I literally cannot contain my excitement when I clamber into the carriage. While the palace may be the stuff of fairytales, it is, to borrow a cliché, a gilded cage. I can barely walk through a corridor without passing a servant who asks if I need anything or a courtier who makes a polite comment but can't mask the confusion on his face.

Oh well. I should be glad that the paparazzi in Athelia have yet to become as annoying as those in our modern world. Here, as cameras are huge, bulky monsters that are outrageously expensive, the chances of any unflattering photos of me appearing in tabloids are low.

Edward also seems to be in a good mood as he settles in the carriage next to me, languorously stretching out his long legs, his mouth curved in a lazy smile. He takes my hand, and I lean against him, savoring the moment. Privacy at last.

"How did you convince the Lord Chamberlain that you had to leave early?" I ask.

"Prior engagement with Henry," he says. "Which is actually the truth. I wished to discuss with him the implementation of the healthcare service you told me about."

"Good—even though that doesn't really give me a legitimate reason to tag along."

"How could I refuse your request when you whistled to me like that?" His voice is subtly shaded with amusement. I flush, recalling how shocked the servants looked. One even dropped a basketful of apples.

"If there were cell phones, I could've called you," I mumble, burrowing my face into his chest. He always smells wonderful— of leather and soap and something distinctly masculine. "Madame Dubois will kill me if she knows."

Now he laughs, a deep, rich sound that rumbles through his chest. A moment later, his arm goes around my back, fitting me into a snugger position against his body.

"It is my fault." A note of regret resonates in his tone. "Because of who I am, you must endure these lessons. Perhaps if I speak to Madame Dubois—"

"No!" I quickly say. It isn't his fault that tradition required that I should train to be a princess. "Don't do that. Moving into the palace is a LOT better than staying at Lady Bradshaw's." And I mean it. I had to endure Lady Bradshaw's scolding, Bianca's snipes and Pierre's exasperation, and with the exception of Martha and Elle, the servants' indifference or even hostility. My only comfort came from books.

Here at the palace, Edward has been everything I could ask for in a boyfriend. He's gone out of his way to ensure that I wouldn't feel out of place, such as defending me in front of courtiers, showering me with books and flowers, and breaking or adapting conventions to accommodate my modern behavior.

"Edward, stop blaming yourself. Being with you is worth facing ten Madame Duboises." Then I lean in and kiss him. In response, he pulls me onto his lap and runs his fingers in my hair, making it impossible for me to pull away, but I don't care.

The temperature seems to go up until the carriage halts. Edward lets me go just before Bertram opens the door, but the latter gives us a grin that hints that he knows we've been making out.

I smooth my hair, lift my chin, and assume a mask of dignified indifference as befitting a princess. Sometimes Madame Dubois's lessons can be useful, after all.

☙❧

THIS ISN'T THE FIRST TIME THAT I'VE GONE TO POPPY'S house. Still, it is usually her visiting me in the palace. Mr. Davenport is often away since he has an internship with a big-name barrister. Sir Montgomery hired a cook, a housekeeper, and a maid for Poppy. Even though he looked murderous when he arrived at Poppy's elopement, he really does love his daughter.

When Edward and I arrive, a maid answers the door and ushers us into a neat, comfortable parlor. Edward declines an offer to take his coat, as he'll be leaving soon to see Henry. When Poppy enters, her hand flies to her mouth, then a huge grin spreads over her face. Sometimes she still seems like a young girl, not an old, matronly married woman.

"Kat! Oh, and Your Highness!" She sweeps into a deep curtsy. "What a wonderful surprise! I was bored out of my life, and I dearly wished to pay you a visit, but Jonathan is adamant that I remain home till I'm fully recovered."

"Is it the morning sickness?" I ask. While she doesn't look as bright and energetic as on the croquet field, she doesn't look pale or sickly at all. "You're not throwing up your food or anything?"

Poppy looks surprised. "How did you know that?"

Uh-oh. Another piece of knowledge that I, from the modern world, am not supposed to know. Even though I've told Poppy that I don't come from Athelia, she hasn't really believed me.

"I . . . I came across it when I was reading a book. You know how much I like to read."

Poppy looks a little puzzled, but then she gestures to the dining room. "Let's sit down, and I'll ask Mary to bring some refreshments for you. Do you prefer coffee or tea, Your Highness?" There is a timid note in her voice as she glances at Edward. He isn't a tyrant, but I guess he might still seem intimidating toward his subjects.

Edward shakes his head. "My apologies, but I must be going. Henry is expecting me." He drops a quick kiss on my head. "I will be back in two hours. Do not leave without me."

When he leaves, Poppy visibly relaxes. She sinks into her chair and lets out a sigh of relief.

I giggle. "You look like an ogre just left."

"I can't help it. He is the prince, after all. When I came to stay with Claire, she couldn't stop talking about him, as though he's a deity sent from heaven."

"Sorry to disappoint you, but he's human. Like you and me."

Poppy grins. "I could tell that he really loves you. There is this smoldering flame in his eyes when he looks at you." She puts a hand on my arm. "I'm so glad that you accepted his proposal, Kat. I know this means you'll have to sacrifice your chance of going back to your family, but we are here for you. We'll be your family."

I smile, touched, but I don't bother to correct her. "Enough about me," I say, bringing out the parcel I've been carrying. "Here—this is for you . . . I mean, when the baby is born."

Poppy protests that there's no need to be so generous, but I place the parcel firmly in her lap. "Open it," I command in a tone that sounds eerily like Edward's. Only a few weeks in the palace, and his authoritative attitude is already rubbing off on me. I'd better watch myself, or I'll turn into someone like Bianca.

She unwraps the parcel and lifts out a delicate white baby dress suitable for a girl or a boy, a lacy nightcap, and a rattle.

"This is so exquisite," Poppy gushes. "Did you make the dress all by yourself, Kat?"

"Yeah, I'm a genius with my needle . . . not. Of course I got someone to make it for me."

"No matter. When the baby is born, you will be his godmother."

Again I give her that fake, too-bright-to-be-sincere smile. By the time the baby is born, I will only have a few months left in Athelia.

I decide to change the subject. There's a book lying on the table—at first I wonder what kind of stories Poppy likes to read, but then at a closer glance I discover it is simply a notebook, the pages scribbled with numbers.

"What have you been doing?" I indicate the notebook.

Poppy rubs her forehead and grimaces. "I've been trying to keep accounts on our household budget. You know, with the baby coming and all, Jonathan said we must record all our expenses. But it's dreadfully hard, Kat."

I remember Mom balancing our checkbook every month, her brow furrowed as she chews on a pencil and taps the buttons on the calculator. "Have you had trouble making the ends meet?"

Poppy shakes her head. "We barely go out for meals and parties, and Papa's offered to provide assistance whenever necessary. Jonathan would prefer not to rely on Papa too much, but he's more willing to accept help since I am with child." She puffs up her cheeks, looking frustrated. "It's the numbers that are darned difficult to keep tabs on; they make my head spin."

If she doesn't spend much, I wonder why she's having difficulty with the numbers. "Can I have a look?"

There's always a mundane side to getting married, I think, as I run a finger down the column Poppy has drawn up. I have to learn an encyclopedia's worth of royal etiquette and customs, while Poppy, whom I suppose you can call a middle-class house-wife, has to deal with adding up the bills for milk, eggs, bacon, bread, sardines, and the like.

"If a pound of sugar costs three shillings, then you'd spend nine shillings for three pounds, not eight." I point out a spot where she made a mistake. "Also, see here. If the grocer gave you a 20 percent discount on a pot of strawberry jam, which costs five shillings, then you should have paid four shillings, not four and a half."

I draw a diagram to illustrate, and Poppy's eyes widen. "And I even thanked him for giving me a big discount! Kat, is there anything you don't know about?"

I mumble something about reading too much.

"I wish Papa had let me read more when I was a child," Poppy says ruefully. "He used to say that trashy novels would corrupt my mind, and he limited my reading to guidebooks for young women."

Given the kind of education I had endured since arriving at Lady Bradshaw's house, I can't say I'm too surprised.

The doorbell rings. The maid gets the door, and in comes a stocky young man and a lovely young woman with honey blond hair and baby blue eyes.

"Jonathan!" Poppy exclaims, rising from her chair. "Look who's come to visit us!"

Mr. Davenport kisses the top of her head and makes her sit down. He gives me a warm, friendly smile and asks how I'm doing. Once, he had bowed to me when he accompanied Poppy to visit me in the palace, but I told—ordered—him to treat me as a friend. I don't think I'll ever get used to this Royal High-ness stuff.

"Good morning, miss." Elle starts to drop into a curtsy, but I stop her.

"It's Kat," I say firmly. "Don't let me catch you saying 'miss' again. You aren't my servant anymore."

Elle lets loose a pretty, tinkling laugh like wind chimes. She takes off her bonnet and hangs it on the rack. She must have been here before, judging by the familiarity with which she moves about the house.

"Mary, get us a fresh pot of tea and bring two more teacups." Poppy leans forward, her eyes bright and inquisitive. "Did the case go well? Do tell us that the judge listened to you!"

Elle nods. She settles on a chair and clasps her hands together. "The judge has ruled that I am indeed the daughter of Earl Bradshaw, and that Madam—Lady Bradshaw—should yield the earl's manor in the country and two-thirds of his fortune to me."

I give an unladylike whoop of joy. Luckily, everyone is too excited about the news to be concerned about my behavior. Poppy claps her hands like a child, while Mr. Davenport grins like he's the one who inherited a fortune.

"I'm so glad for you, Elle. Now you won't have to worry about your mother and Billy, and Lady Petunia won't have further reason to object your, um, association with Henry."

She doesn't look as overjoyed as we are. "I'm afraid his mother still needs convincing."

"But it's proven that you are the daughter of an earl," I say. "What more does she have against you?"

Elle shakes her head. "I am no longer a servant, but that doesn't mean she thinks I am good enough for Henry. There are plenty of better choices than me."

"But it's you he wants," I say.

Poppy nods fiercely. "You deserve each other."

The maid brings us a steaming teapot. Elle pours herself a cup and takes a sip before speaking.

"I want to wait a while. I want to make sure that what Henry feels for me isn't simply an infatuation."

Somehow I am reminded of Mr. Bingley (Henry) and Jane Bennet (Elle). Only in this case, Darcy (Edward) isn't scheming to separate them, and Henry's mother resembles Lady Catherine de Burgh.

"Besides, everything happened so fast." Elle pinches her bottom lip and looks downward. For a moment she looks lost, vulnerable, afraid. I feel like giving Henry a good shake for making her feel this insecure. "It's only a few months ago that I left the Bradshaws' and started working at the palace. Then I learn that I'm the daughter of an earl, and suddenly I'm an heiress?" She shakes her head and releases a deep breath. "All I want now is to take some time and think it over. There are some things I know I need to do—I want to send Billy to school and have Mamsie quit working. Or at least buy her a sewing machine; we've never been able to afford one."

"If you need further assistance with legal matters, I will be happy to provide it," Mr. Davenport says. "I can also refer you to an accountant if you need one. Anything I can do for a friend and cousin."

Elle smiles at him gratefully. "You have done so much for me already. All of you."

"Well, I'd say if the duchess remains adamant, there's always Ruby Red." Poppy smirks, her eyes twinkling.

Elle looks scandalized, but Mr. Davenport laughs. I laugh as well, but I can't help feeling a bit sympathetic for her. I had assumed that once Elle regained her title, she would no longer be considered inferior to Henry, but after encountering Lady Petunia, it's unlikely that Cinderella's fairytale ending is going to arrive soon.

5

I sit on the balcony, half-concealed behind a polished oak pillar. I'm swathed in a dark silk dress, which makes me look at least five years older. Black elbow-length gloves, a black lace veil, and a black fan complete my outfit. The whole ensemble gives me an eerie sense of being like some Gothic romance heroine. It's actually kind of fun, if you ignore the fact that the reason for the costume is that a woman isn't supposed to be here. I'm in the Chamber, where the members of the parliament (MPs, as Edward tells me) gather for the last session. Second-to-last session, to be exact, as the last session, normally known as prorogation, consists merely of a summary of the year's achievements.

Like the palace, the Chamber is a breathtaking construction. It adheres to the red and gold theme of Athelia's monarchy, with a magnificent golden ceiling and throne, while rows of red leather seats line up before the throne. Above the throne are huge paintings depicting famous monarchs. I recognize most of them, thanks to my industrious studying under Madame Dubois. Behind me, stained-glass windows rise to the ceiling, casting daylight into the room. As it's rather cloudy today, the four golden chandeliers are lit to compensate for the lack of sufficient lighting.

Because it's so ▇▇▇ stifling in my Gothic costume, I start to fan myself. If the MPs notice me, then so be it.

Edward appears in a formal black suit and trousers, carrying a scroll tied with a red ribbon. He strides to the throne and waits for the members to quiet down. His steadfast gaze and straight posture remind me that although Athelia is a constitutional monarchy, he still carries himself with this majestic, commanding air. Most of the members cease their chatter and sit in silence, their gaze fixed upon the prince. It's kind of a double standard for me, because while I don't hesitate to let Edward know I will never behave like a spineless subject, I find it amusing that the MPs are subdued in his presence.

After Edward presents an opening speech, which sounds just like a boring recital, the Prime Minister goes up to the podium and gives an annual report from various departments and agencies. He is a dumpy man wearing a wig—the long, fake, white kind worn by judges in civil court. It's a pity Edward doesn't have to wear a wig, because I'd certainly die of laughter. Then several MPs come forth to deliver local and national presentations of papers, all of which sound extremely dry and tedious.

Just when I'm in danger of falling asleep, the Prime Minister adjusts his glasses and reads from a scroll.

"Now let us commence the Third Reading of the eight-hour bill. For those who wish to express an opinion, will you please raise your hand?"

I sit up and lean forward in my chair, my heart pounding. Edward had told me that with a landslide victory in the Second Reading, plus the growing attention from the public and continued reports from investigators and novelists, it is hardly probable that the Third Reading will be rejected. Still, it doesn't mean that all members will cheerfully pass the bill without further comment. Several MPs are invested in the cotton trade, which is considered one of the largest industries of Athelia.

A man raises his hand and is granted permission to speak. He is quite passionate about the bill, stating that eight hours is still too much that any child can bear. He cites evidence from a medical report written by Dr. Jensen, whom I remember is Henry's mentor.

"I would even go further and propose that the working hours should be reduced to half a day in the morning, which leaves the afternoon free for mandatory education."

I could hug him, if it weren't that I was supposed to stay out of sight.

Another man stands up and expresses an opposing opinion. He says that with the rapid advancement of technology, Athelia has transformed into the most powerful nation in the world. The country will fall behind if the supply cannot keep up with demand. While he acknowledges that there are problems with the child workers, he is confident that as long as the children are carefully monitored and no violence is inflicted upon them, there is no reason why the factories cannot continue as before.

████████. I wonder if he has ever been inside a factory himself.

The debate continues for a while, but much to my disappointment, it looks like the hours cannot be further reduced. Most of the members, while willing to concede that it's harmful for children to work long hours, are also unwilling to cut down the hours from twelve to four. Edward wasn't kidding when he told me that the parliament is reluctant to drastic change.

Edward puts up his hand, causing everyone to stop squabbling right away. "I propose amendments to go with the bill," he says, instead of arguing for further reduction of the hours. "Inspectors must be appointed to ensure that the working conditions are at least tolerable, and heavy fines must be enforced should the factory owners fail to comply with the rules."

"Given the sheer number of factories in the nation, where would the salaries for those inspectors come from?" someone asks rather nastily. "You can hardly believe that our coffers are bottomless!"

"Then we can raise the taxes on the factory managers." Edward's voice is as cool as the early morning air. He has never used the same tone with me, however. Sometimes I wonder if I should appreciate how neatly he manages to separate his public image (cold, distant, aloof) from private (caring, teasing, affectionate). "After all, it is their responsibility to ensure the safety of their own employees."

An image of Andrew McVean flashes in my mind. I remember how he acted like a complete jerk when I told him about Jimmy's death. Before I know it, I am on my feet.

Because it is so quiet in the room, when I stand up and my chair makes a horrible scraping noise, everyone is staring at me. Most of them, who aren't expecting my presence, stare at me in utter amazement.

I should duck under the balustrade and pretend I was a ghost and that they were merely hallucinating. But Edward had told me that Parliament will not be in session until next year, so I won't be able to voice my opinion until several months later. And I still can't forget Jimmy's blood-soaked pillow, as well as Mrs. Thatcher and Elle weeping silently in that dark, gloomy room. Like their future is doomed. Even if I become a laughingstock, I at least need to let my voice be heard.

"I . . . I'm terribly sorry . . ." I stammer, tightening my hands over the folds of my dress to keep myself steady. I'm on the second floor, so I have to raise my voice, and because they are so shocked into silence, most people seem to be able to hear me. "But I thought if you don't mind . . . I have a few suggestions to make."

My voice grows stronger. It's easier when I'm not looking at their faces. I stare straight ahead and ignore any negative thoughts of what might happen or what consequences there could be from my speaking out.

"We need compensation. Because the environment is so dangerous, I highly recommend that compensation be offered to all children who are seriously injured or . . . deceased. And they must have healthcare. The employer should invest in health insurance so they will be able to afford the medical bills. Oh, and sick leave. If they cannot come to work because they are ill, there should be some form of payment . . ."

"Thank you, Lady Katriona." Edward cuts me off. His voice is curt, clipped, and he doesn't look in my direction. "My apologies, everyone, but my fiancée is merely reminding me what I have forgotten to mention. If you would also take what she has told us into account . . ."

"That would not be a problem," the Prime Minister says, obviously relieved that Edward had intervened. "Might I ask you to elaborate, Your Highness?"

Edward explains to them in further detail what I had told him about our modern rules. The other MPs start to offer their opinions, seeming to have forgotten my presence completely.

I sink back into my chair and wipe cold sweat from my brow. Part of me is irritated that Edward had simply used my ideas as his own, but part of me is also grateful that he had come to my aid. The MPs could have forcefully ejected me from the room.

6

The cool autumn air drifts in through the window, cooling my cheeks and clearing my head, which is kind of woolly from studying the heavy leather-bound book on my table. I thought I was done when we finished the book on royal etiquette, but Madame Dubois revealed to me that it is in fact only the first book in the series. Great.

I yawn and stretch my arms over my head, and wince when my corset strains against my ribs. Since my outburst in the parliament, Madame Dubois forbade me to go out, including those "lessons in horticulture" in Edward's garden. Needless to say, she was simply furious with me. Her husband is one of the MPs, so she was among the first to learn of my idiotic behavior. Her rage erupted like a volcano, her words spilling like molten lava, burning through my mind.

"Do you realize what you have done, you immature, head-strong girl? I already specifically *told* you that you cannot do as you please. What possessed you to go to the king and beg him for permission for you to enter Parliament? Women have no business in political affairs, as I have drilled into your head countless times. And now you have to go and interrupt the session when the men were discussing important matters! Have you considered how ashamed His Highness would be? Have you considered how the king might feel about your taking advantage of his generous offer and squandering it? Honestly, I simply cannot understand why His Highness chose you as his bride. Athelia has never seen a worse princess than you."

I don't even feel like defending myself. I'm no longer the younger, less attractive, socially inept sister in the Bradshaw household. It wouldn't matter so much if I only had myself to blame, but now my stupid impetuosity will reflect badly on the king and Edward.

Edward has been surprisingly lenient, but it doesn't make me feel much better. "Kat, don't take it to heart. I admit that it was thoughtless to shout out in the middle of the session, but since it has already happened, what matters more is that you have repented and are doing penitence. Besides, if a MP is more concerned about your manners than your ideas, which are excellent, then it does not speak highly of his character. I would not worry about such a man's opinion."

I wish he had shown more displeasure. I know how much criticism he had to deal with since I moved into the palace, and I feel like punching myself for letting him defend me so many times. No matter how much I try, my behavior will never be compatible for a conventional princess. Of course, my unusual character is precisely why Edward loves me, but unfortunately, most people at court don't share the same perspective.

I sigh and turn the page, trying to memorize how to greet ambassadors in seven different languages.

"Miss Elle has requested a meeting with you." Amelie pokes her head in. "Miss Poppy is with her."

"They have come together?" I say, surprised. Elle is usually busy with her job and taking care of her family, and Poppy is, well, pregnant. It isn't frequent that they can visit me, not to mention both. "But Madame Dubois might not . . ."

"I'll keep watch for Madame Dubois. They said it won't take long."

I giggle. "Oh, Amelie, I love you."

"Save that confession for His Highness."

Elle enters, neatly dressed in a simple white frock, looking sweet and angelic as usual. She hasn't completely lost her meekness though, from the hesitant way she steps through the door. Poppy also seems a bit nervous. But once she sees me, a huge grin breaks over her face and it feels like every moment that we have a girl talk over hot chocolate.

"Sit down, both of you." I wave them to a sofa and call for a maid to bring refreshments. "Poppy, are there any foods you should avoid while you're pregnant? Actually, how did Mr. Davenport let you come?"

"I haven't thrown up these days, and it's so awfully boring in the house." Poppy grins. "So when Elle told me that she's coming to see you, I begged Jonathan to allow me this one time. He trusts that Elle will take excellent care of me."

"How are you doing, Kat?" Elle says, looking concerned. "From what Henry told me, it seems that you are having a hard time learning to be a princess."

"Oh, I'm all right. Just a lot to learn, that's all." I gesture toward the heavy volume that Madame Dubois made me read. I love books, but textbooks are an exception.

A frown mars Elle's pretty features. "Lady Petunia also insisted I study the very same book. It's awfully difficult when I can barely read and write."

I stare at her. "But how did you work at Lady Bradshaw's if you didn't know how to read?"

"I can handle simple phrases and names," she says simply. "But this is a whole book, and it uses so many big words. I've been asking Cousin Poppy to help me."

I understand. As a matter of fact, I'm pretty sure that half of my classmates back in high school won't be able to read the stuff I've been forced to consume. The books in Athelia, unsurprisingly, are written in an old-fashioned style reminiscent of Dickens or Austen.

"That's the reason why we've come to see you." Poppy says, popping the last bit of a blueberry muffin in her mouth. She has finished an entire plate of muffins in a short while. I suppose it's because her baby is hungry.

I didn't understand. Surely she can't expect me to form a study group.

"Because of my sudden good fortune, I have been able to quit my job at the palace," Elle says, smiling. "I could focus on other things. So I plan to use a portion of my inheritance to fund the opening of a school for girls."

"For all girls, regardless of their status," Poppy adds excitedly. "So girls like me will be able to learn useful subjects, not just how to pour tea and walk backwards with a train."

"That sounds like an awesome—I mean, wonderful—idea," I say.

"Kat," Elle clasps her hands together and looks at me in earnest. "I know you have been really busy, but could you spare a few hours to speak for us?"

"What do you mean?"

Elle explains. She has found an old building in the city center, not far from the Royal Institute where Henry attends his medical lectures, which can be converted into a new school building. But to do that, as well as finding teachers and advertising for pupils, it's going to be a long, arduous task.

"I thought . . . if you could give a speech for those who are rich and powerful, such as the Prime Minister, we might gain more sponsors to establish the school."

Yeah, right. After the session, I heard Edward apologizing to the Prime Minister, who called me brash, naïve, and outrageous. I can still remember how he looked—his lips pinched together and his voice strained.

"I can't." my answer comes out faster than I expected. "I'm sorry, but I doubt they would listen to me, especially after the way I interrupted the parliament."

"Henry told me about it." Elle nods. "You might have broken the protocol, but your ideas are sound. He said that Parliament would benefit more from your ideas. Which is why they need an educated woman like you to speak on behalf of our school."

"Besides, you're the princess." Poppy's eyes are shining. "There's no one better than you, Kat, to show your support for us. You have the power to convince others."

"I . . . let me think about it."

I *am* sympathetic towards Elle and Poppy. I really want to help them with the school. But given my recent record in the parliament, I doubt anyone would want to listen to me. And what would they say to Edward if I came out and expressed these radical ideas? Unlike child labor, I doubt girls' education could rouse the same support from the upper-class, much less the lower-class.

Not to mention that I have to leave Athelia eventually.

7

"We have received a message from Philip," the king says, passing a long, cream-colored envelope to Edward. "It is addressed to you."

"Which Philip?" I whisper to Edward. There are actually six or seven people named Philip among Edward's relatives. The royal family is pretty unimaginative when it comes to names.

"My eldest cousin. Currently the Duke of Northport." Edward scans the letter. "He is inviting Kat and me to his country estate."

"Why now?" the queen says. "We have sent him an invitation for the day of your official engagement."

"He fell off his horse and broke his leg and therefore cannot attend. He has, however, expressed a great desire to see Kat."

I halt in the middle of spreading butter on bread. Engagement. Ever since Edward told me that the wedding would be held in nine months, I knew that the engagement would come sooner or later. Still, it doesn't mean that I'm mentally prepared for it.

I'm having breakfast with the royal family—a ritual I dreaded at first but gradually came to enjoy. No matter how busy we may be, the king insists on dining together as a family. Sometimes Parliament and social functions interfere, but generally, breakfast is one meal we can share.

"Katriona looks like she has swallowed an egg whole," the king says, a questioning look in his eyes. "Have you anything to suggest about the engagement?"

"Um . . ." I set down the butter knife. At first I consider saying no, but then I feel I should know what I'm getting into. "Pardon me, but I've never been engaged before, so what should I be prepared for?"

The king and queen exchange benevolent smiles. Edward gives my hand a quick squeeze under the table.

"According to the Royal Marriage Act," the king says, "I will first announce to the privy council my formal approval of your marriage to my son. Then we will have a small lunch gathering in the Red Room, where the exchange of gifts will take place. Each of you will give a speech."

"Gifts?" I thought only the couple received gifts. No one said anything about an exchange.

"Traditionally, the groom will present a ring," the queen says. "But it is not required for the bride, although if you wish, you may certainly do so."

Edward whispers in my ear. "Don't worry about it."

I decide to get him something anyway. I have my own private income from the proceeds of writing the article on factory children. The article sold thousands of copies, but I've donated most of it to charities since I don't lack anything in the palace. I'll see what I can get with the remaining money.

The king and queen talk on about what we should wear on the engagement day, who to invite for the dinner and dance in the evening, and how many official photos should be taken . . . details that I take in but don't dwell on.

It's happening. Me, officially becoming a princess: Princess of Athelia.

Yeah, right. It's a role I wish I could play, but circumstances prevent me from making it permanent. No matter how much I want to stay, I can't.

I finish my bread with the help of a full glass of milk. Then I ask to be excused, curtsy, and head toward my room.

Edward catches up with me in one of the many corridors. "Kat," he says, his tone filled with concern. His hand closes over my wrist. "Kat, wait."

I turn around, a bright smile pasted on my face. "I told you I'm fine. Seriously."

"It is not your own nervousness that you are concerned about."

He knows.

"Edward, I . . ."

He sighs and holds out his arms, but he drops them when a few servants rush by. No intimacy is allowed in the palace, at least not when there's an audience.

"What did we agree to that day in my garden?"

"To make the remaining days I have with you the happiest you have ever lived," I whisper. There's a lump in my throat and I keep my gaze anywhere but on his face.

"And you are not upholding your side of the promise."

"I know." My voice is normal, but I feel like shouting in the corridor. "But this isn't fair to you! I wish I didn't have to go. I'm not going to be queen, and there's no way I can make it up to you."

"Kat, don't—"

"I wish there were someone for you," I say savagely. I clench my fists and let go. "If only there were someone who could make you happy after I . . ."

He silences me with a fingertip on my lips. "Say no more. I knew the consequences, and I'm willing to go through this. Even if it means you must leave me eventually."

"I'm not worth it."

"For me, you are."

My breath catches in my throat. He's not helping things a bit. He's only making me feel worse.

Edward caresses my cheek, his palm warm against my skin. "Listen to me, Kat. I am well aware that you feel guilty about leaving me behind. Most likely I would feel the same if I were in your place. But after all the effort of trying to make you love me . . . now that I finally have you, my only wish is that our moments together will not be wasted. We certainly shouldn't spend our time devising another woman for me; it will only cause pain for both of us. Do not ever, mention finding someone; I do not want to hear of it again. Now"—he plants a lightning-fast kiss on my forehead—"go back to your room and ask Amelie to commence packing. Philip expects us in a few days."

❧ 8 ❧

"I'd give anything to see what they are doing up there," I whisper.

"I doubt there is much to see. Bertram has rarely managed to form more than one coherent sentence when he talks to Amelie. However, I confess that I share your sentiment."

The carriage rumbles on the road, taking us on the journey to Northport. Edward and I sit together, my head on his lap, his fingers playing idly in my hair. Strictly speaking, Amelie should be riding with us, but Edward ordered her to sit outside on the box with Bertram. She had obeyed him without question. I felt a little guilty for making her leave, but the look of hope on Bertram's face silenced me.

I can't help feeling more cheerful now that we are leaving the palace. No stuffy lessons with Madame Dubois, no servants hanging around every corner I turn. Edward and I can have more chances to spend some quality time alone together. And I'm curious to see Northport. The queen told me that Duke Philip—I mean, Cousin Philip—enjoys a leisurely, luxurious life in the country, and his house is possibly the most beautiful one of all the country estates.

"How long has Bertram had a crush—how long has he liked Amelie?" With nothing else to do in the carriage, I'm in the mood for gossip.

"She came to replace a servant who was old enough to retire, but Bertram has known her since they were children since the two families have known each other for a long time. I cannot fix the exact time when he started behaving like a fool around her."

"Their families know each other already?"

"Both their families have served us for generations back."

I process the information in my mind. This is something new to me. "Are the children of their families free to choose other careers?"

"Certainly; they have the liberty to choose whatever path they prefer, but it is much easier to simply follow their parents' footsteps. And compared to the risk of making a living in trade or being an apprentice for years, working at the palace is a relatively attractive prospect. Room and board are covered, and the pay is stable."

"I suppose so. If you put it that way." I shift my position and yelp. Several hairpins jab into my scalp. "If they knew each other for so long, I wonder why Bertram hasn't done anything to show his interest. Surely he can't be content to simply admire her from afar."

"He has tried to display his affection, but unfortunately, it turned out to be a tragedy."

I sit up. "Tell me," I demand.

"There was one day that Bertram came to the greenhouse and asked Galen if he could put together a bouquet before autumn sets in. Since Bertram never expressed an interest in flowers, Galen was naturally curious and asked him the purpose. At first Bertram was too embarrassed to admit that he wanted to give Amelie flowers—he made up a story about decorating his window—but I wormed the truth from him."

"And why is that a tragedy?"

The corners of his mouth curve up. "Amelie is allergic to flowers. She was sneezing all the way to the hospital ward when she left him."

"That's too bad," I say, but I also can't help feeling amused. "Bertram should have done his homework before he tried to give her a present."

Edward puts his hand over mine. "I'm glad that you aren't allergic to flowers, or we'll only have the storage room left for a secret tryst."

Here is one instance that I get all tongue-tied, as memories flood in my mind. During the ball, Bianca tried to go after Edward with a pair of magic-infused gloves. In a hasty decision, I shoved Edward inside a tiny storage room for cleaning supplies, which resulted in a passionate make-out session that would have made headlines if anyone had found us. To this day, I can't pass that room without a sting of embarrassment.

Not long after, we have to stop to let the horses rest. When I emerge from the carriage, Amelie lets out a noise of frustration and signals to me. She leads me a little way off from the procession and whips out a brush.

"Tell His Highness to stop running his fingers in your hair." She pulls the pins out and lets my hair fall past my back. "I've lost count of the occasions I've had to re-fashion your hair. At the very least, don't allow him to mess up your hair before you have to look presentable."

Embarrassed, I fiddle with the lace on my sleeves. "Sorry."

"By the way, I thought that you should know that Miss Elle won't be joining us in Northport."

"Why not?" I remember Edward mentioning that she did get an invitation.

"She sent word that she had to look for qualified teachers

for the girls' school. I didn't get the message until it was late, and I didn't want to wake you up."

Oh well. I suppose that can't be helped; knowing Elle, she would much prefer to do something more useful than attending parties. I wish I could do the same, but the invitation is aimed primarily at me.

I grip my elbows, feeling disappointed. Sure, I have Edward with me, but I'd like some female company as well. On the other hand, it might be just as well she can't come. The duchess and Henry are bound to be there, and I'm sure Elle would feel horribly out of place and awkward if Lady Petunia is also present.

When Edward learns that Elle is not going to show up, he falls silent for a moment, his expression pensive.

"Is there something wrong?" I ask. "You look so serious."

He rubs the middle of his forehead. "Do you know what usually happens in autumn for the aristocracy?"

"A lot of them go back to the country, since Parliament is closed."

"What would you do if you were cooped up in a huge mansion without all the excitement and parties going on in the capital during summer?"

"Um . . ."

"Why, you would hold your own parties at your house. It is impossible that my cousin would only invite Henry and me. Considering my cousin's love of society, I estimate that there will be at least 20 to 30 nobles waiting for us to arrive."

I feel my heart sinking. "After all the fuss and bustle of the Season?"

"As a matter of fact, September and October are also known as the Little Season. Some mothers would try to secure a match if their daughters did not succeed in procuring a proposal in the main Season. That's why I am particularly concerned for Henry.

No doubt the duchess hopes to find him another girl so his ardor for Elle will cool down."

My head is swimming. I thought it was going to be a simple gathering of meeting his cousin. I didn't sign up for another Season. Even though there's no pressure now to find a husband, it doesn't mean that I'm ready for another round of balls and parties and socializing.

"In Athelia, if a man is found in a compromising position with a woman, he is often obligated to marry her to protect her reputation. Of course, this unwritten rule isn't always enforced, but with Lady Petunia so keen on finding someone else for Henry, if there's a suitable girl who is found alone with him . . . well, there is the possibility that he may cave in to pressure." Edward turns my chin, making me look at him. There is no smile on his face at all. "In fact . . . I may as well warn you that both of us might also need to watch ourselves. It is unlikely, but not impossible, that some people have not completely relinquished the hope of becoming queen."

I stare at him. "But we're practically engaged!"

"I have made my intentions quite clear at the ball, but the fact remains that the formal ceremony has yet to take place." He holds up my hand and brushes his fingers across my bare knuckles. As I try to avoid wearing too much jewelry, there's nothing on my hands or wrists. "Neither of us wears an engagement ring yet. I wished to wait until our engagement was over to visit Cousin Philip, but it seems that he has broken his leg at a very opportune moment."

His hand tightens on my arm. "Promise me, Kat. If a man requests your company with him alone, do not follow him."

I highly doubt that is going to happen, plus it's much more likely that he will be cornered by eager girls, but I nod and squeeze his hand. "I promise."

And to think I was looking forward to this trip. It sounds more like a nightmare.

9

Pemberley. That's the first thing that comes to mind when we arrive at the country estate. Our carriage halts on a hill, and from there, I glimpse a museum-like building that is handsome, grand, and very like Pemberley in the Jane Austen movie. There's even a sparkling lake right in front of it, surrounded by fir trees. Surreptitiously, I glance at Edward's pristine white shirt peeking from his dark coat and look away quickly.

"Pray tell me what is preying on your mind," he says, a gleam in his hazel eyes. "I confess that every time you have a guilty look on your face, it amuses me and makes me wonder what outlandish notion has sprung up in that unconventional head of yours."

"Nothing."

He chucks my chin playfully, the heat from his skin warm against mine. "Out with it."

But I'm not ready to confess the fangirl part of my twenty-first-century mind. And even if I were, what are the chances of him jumping into the lake?

I search wildly for a different topic. "So, what is your cousin like?"

"Philip? Someone whom I was expected to emulate."

"What are you supposed to be like, then?" I mean, come on. Even if Philip's shortcomings are very few, I should think Athelia could hardly ask for a better leader.

Edward absentmindedly plays with my fingers and releases a deep breath. "Cousin Philip is, in many ways, my complete opposite. He is sociable, gregarious, and makes friends easily. And he excels at sports."

"But you are athletic," I say incredulously, eyeing his muscular chest with fangirl approval. Although I have yet to see Edward half naked, I can testify that he has a mouth-watering physique. Every time I see him working in the greenhouse or in his private garden with his sleeves rolled up to his elbows and his shirt gaping to reveal a sheen of sweat on his collarbone, I still cannot prevent a deep blush creeping up my skin. He had tried to conceal his laughter and even casually told me that he should prance around shirtless just to see me flush and fidget.

"I should modify that to team sports. I am afraid that I never took pleasure in rugby or cricket or football. I preferred the more solitary pleasures of archery and boxing. I simply do not work well in groups. Additionally, much of my strength is gained from shoveling earth and carrying flowerpots."

I picture Edward playing football with a group of rowdy young men. No, I can't imagine him whooping or bellowing or yelling. He's the kind who won't follow orders; he prefers to go ahead and do things himself.

"I guess that your cousin Philip didn't play much with you when you were children."

"Actually, Philip is more than ten years my senior, so he used to take the role of an instructor instead. He meant well, I suppose, but try as I might, I couldn't be like him. I am sure that you have noticed I am no socialite."

"Neither am I." Which is perfectly fine, I want to say. If he were this playboy prince who loved to throw parties and balls, I wouldn't have fallen in love with him.

"When I was younger," Edward says as he closes his eyes briefly, "there were times that I wished that Philip was heir to the throne, for he has fulfilled everything expected of a prince. He revels in interacting with large groups of people. And in addition to his easygoing character, he also married early to a most suitable woman and now has two sons and a daughter."

"Who cares about him?" I say, earning a smirk from him. "I know you and your character, Edward. You are perfect."

He raises his eyebrows.

"Not all the time," I hastily amend, "but I love you just the way you are."

He looks like he wants to kiss me again, but he doesn't move. I wonder why—he rarely held back during previous occasions, but when I glance at the window, I understand why he's restraining himself. The road leading up to the entrance of the duke's house is flanked with crowds of villagers. The men have tweed caps similar to Ponytail Godfrey's while the women wear aprons with dark gowns. Several children are also present, carrying bouquets of flowers.

"Long live His Highness! Long live Her Highness!"

I grab Edward's arm. "These people . . . they are cheering for our arrival?"

"I should think it obvious. They certainly are not here for Bertram."

"But there's so many of them!"

"It is not what I enjoy," he says with the air of a man resigned to the inevitable, "but I have no influence over what my cousin wishes to do."

"Is this common—telling the people they have to line up and welcome us?"

"It is usual for tenants to defer to a lord in return for the food baskets and medicine sent to them in aid. From what I've heard, Constance is used to having the village women curtsy to her whenever she visits."

I press my lips together. I know I should be used to the way royals are treated by now, but deep down inside, that modern part of me still squirms with discomfort. I haven't done anything except catch the attention of the prince. And here are groups of people who never heard about me before, clapping and cheering as though I've saved the world.

Edward gets off the carriage first and offers his hand. I place my hand in his and step out, taking great care not to trip in front of so many people.

"Your Highness." A young girl curtsies to me and holds out a cluster of baby-pink roses. "This is for you."

I accept the roses with a smile. "Thank you."

"Edward." A deep, pleasant voice carries through the cool autumn air. A man with a well-trimmed beard limps toward us. He doesn't use a walking stick or cane for support—I guess that's why he has another man trailing behind, looking tense and apprehensive.

"My little cousin, all grown up, bringing his chosen bride along for a visit. How wonderful it is to finally meet the lovely girl who has stolen my cousin's heart." He extends a hand to me. I have been instructed on the etiquette of greeting male relatives, so I give the brightest smile I can muster and take his hand. "It is a great pleasure to meet you as well, Cousin Philip. Edward has spoken highly of you."

He leans towards me and waggles his eyebrows, as though I'm a kid. "Don't listen to him. Anything flattering he paints of me is untrue."

Then he gestures to a woman dressed in a fine brocaded gown. She's beautiful—flawless porcelain skin, doll-like features, and pale-blond hair expertly coiffed and perfumed. She is no young girl, but I can tell she has gone to great lengths to maintain her youth. "Allow me to introduce my wife, Lady Constance, Duchess of Northport."

I am beginning to curtsy when I remind myself that I'm ranked higher than Constance. I quickly withdraw my hands from the thick folds of my gown and thread my fingers together at my stomach. I incline my head—gracefully, I hope—and smile.

"I am very happy to make your acquaintance, Constance."

The woman returns a smile, gracious and polite, though she glances briefly at her husband. I've no idea what that glance conveys, but from the fleeting lift of eyebrows, it doesn't seem to be flattering. Maybe she's thinking that the prince's fiancée really is as ordinary as the rumors say.

But once she opens her mouth, her voice flows over us like honey. "Absolutely delighted to meet you, my dear. Do come in." Constance embraces me, and I catch the scent of bergamot oil. "Our party is not complete without you."

I look back at the villagers, still lined up on both sides of the road. I can't even see the little girl who gave me flowers. Of course, they aren't invited to the party.

Edward lays a hand on my elbow, indicating we should go inside. Servants hold the doors open, take our coats, and usher us through a long, handsomely furnished hall. Having seen the palace's splendor, I'm not particularly impressed with Philip's house, but the number of servants flitting around us makes me a bit dizzy. They all look the same—men in dark shirts and pants, women in black dresses and white aprons. Philip and Constance probably don't have to do anything all day except to lift a finger or bark a command.

At the end of the hall is another set of heavy doors. My stomach gets fluttery at the sight of the crowd of well-dressed people seated in an enormous living room. There's Claire Fremont—breathtakingly lovely as usual—sitting with her mother, and several others with whom I was acquainted during the Season. I've met them while playing croquet at Claire's, or they're friends I have called on with Bianca. There's even a girl that looks familiar—I recognize her as the one who shrieked and jumped when Krev let loose a mouse at the ball. And finally I spot Henry. He looks relieved when he sees us. Next to him, the duchess has an annoyed look on her face, which immediately vanishes when I meet her eye.

"Ladies and gentlemen," Philip says, barely concealing the excitement in his voice as though he is presenting an exotic animal in a zoo. "Our most honorable Highness and his bride have traveled all the way from the capital and come to join our company."

There is a flurry of movement. Skirts rustle and people smooth their hair. The members of the aristocracy stand up and bow or curtsy. *I could get used to this*, then I mentally smack myself. I will be leaving eventually, and there is no reason to be happy about people paying their respects merely because I'm tied to a royal family.

Edward squeezes my hand. I have received guests in the palace before, but this is the first time I've had to deal with so many people. I swallow and try to arrange myself to look as calm and gracious as Constance. Even though I have been in large gatherings before, I am used to being ignored—keeping everyone's ears safe from my piano playing and singing. Now, there is no escape as everyone's attention is on the prince and me.

Philip and Constance lead us around the room, introducing us to Lord so-and-so, Lady so-and-so—names that I can barely remember. My mind is already jammed from learning Edward's ancestors. I'm glad for Edward's hand on my arm. His touch is warm and comforting, his presence a pillar of security.

Lady Fremont and Claire greet me with wide, sunny smiles. In the past, they kept their focus on my sister. They looked at me with disdain or not at all. I can't help deriving a small vindictive pleasure at being the center of attention now.

Henry's greeting is more warm and genuine, but I can feel his gaze darting behind me, as though I am concealing someone. When Edward engages the duchess's attention by talking about some trivial detail of our engagement, I tell Henry: "Elle can't join us here. I'm sorry—she has been super busy these days."

He stiffens for a second, though his smile doesn't waver. Henry may be more approachable compared to Edward, but growing up as one of Edward's cousins, he also knows how to mask his emotions when necessary. "I had expected something like this. Is it about the school for girls that she plans to open?"

"She told you already?"

Henry darts a glance at his mother, then speaks in a low voice. "She has asked if I could convince a few instructors at the Royal Institute to teach a few courses at her school."

"Wow." I'm impressed at Elle's efficiency and resourcefulness. "She really is set on opening that school." I rub my elbows and feel a pang of guilt for declining her request that I voice support for girls' education.

This time, Henry's cheerfulness vanishes. There is a pained, almost forlorn look in his eyes. "She certainly is. She might seem gentle and soft-hearted, but she possesses a determined, single-minded resolution when faced with difficulties. It is an admirable quality, but sometimes I think she cares more for . . ."

"Henry," the duchess lays a hand on her son's arm, then glances at me. "I do apologize for interrupting, but there are some people we were going to speak to before you arrived. It would not do to keep them waiting."

There is a challenging note in her tone and look. Henry opens his mouth for a second, but no sound comes out. With a triumphant grin, the duchess steers him away. I wish I could yank her hand off and tell her to stop interfering in her son's love life, but what can I say when Henry allows himself to be trodden on?

"Let him alone, Kat," Edward whispers in my ear. "If he is truly attached to Elle, he will not disappoint her."

"He'd better," I say fervently, though at the same time I also wonder what Henry had meant to tell me. Does he mean that he believes that Elle cares more for her charity efforts than for him?

A while later, I wish I could retire to a room. We have spent the whole day traveling. I long to throw off the heavy gown I'm wearing. If this socializing goes on, I will have to tape my eyelids to stop them from closing. Wait—this world doesn't have plastic tape. Yet.

Edward seems to sense my weariness. "Cousin," he says in a low voice. "My apologies, but we would request for a while to rest and change. It has been a long day."

Philip doesn't look too concerned. "Pshaw, it's not even five o'clock! Surely our Princess Katriona is capable of greeting her subjects. It's not that taxing compared to those balls that last until early morning. A cup of strong coffee will help restore her spirits."

"At least stay a while longer to meet the children," Constance quickly says, seeing that Edward is narrowing his eyes. "They have been longing to see their Uncle Ed. And, of course, to meet Katriona."

She hails a servant, ordering that the children be brought to the sitting room. I look up at Edward and raise my eyebrows. "Uncle Ed?"

He remains impassive, but I think I detect a glimmer in his eyes. "Is that a problem?"

"It hardly suits you. An uncle should be hearty and jolly and present a fatherly image—not that broody, moody person I see."

"No stranger than Aunt Kat."

I make a face at him. This time he smiles; I feel like recording it as a victory. Uncle Ed and Aunt Kat—I have to admit the names sound good, even though it feels way too early to be thought of as an elder relative.

Presently, the servant returns with a boy and a girl. They march, almost like the children in The Sound of Music, their postures as stiff as bricks. But their eyes—large and expressive like their parents'—gaze at me with eagerness and curiosity.

"Darlings," Constance says, taking them by the hand and pushing them forward. "Uncle Ed has finally decided to get married! Isn't it exciting? And he's brought his bride to see you."

Edward loops an arm around my shoulder. "Say hello to Aunt Kat."

Constance gestures to the boy, who looks about twelve or thirteen. "This is Thomas, my second oldest." He touches a hand to his forelock and nods at me like a well-trained soldier. "And this is Liana Rose, but we all call her Rosie." The girl doesn't look older than ten. She's a small, dainty thing who reminds me of that glass shepherdess on the mantelpiece when I still lived at Lady Bradshaw's house. No wonder she's called Rosie.

I wink at her, and she gives a tiny smile, which she quickly covers up with a delicate white hand. I feel as though I've met someone I can be totally comfortable with.

"By the way, where is Tristan?" Edward says. It's then that I recall he told me that Philip and Constance have three children.

"He's still away at boarding school—they have a huge rowing competition this week." Constance shakes her head. "The older he is, the less he listens to his old mother."

Just then, a servant rushes up to Philip. "Lady Lillie has just arrived."

A girl attired in a pristine white dress enters the room. She has the prettiest eyes I've ever seen, which curve into crescent moons when she smiles. Although her dress is simple, and she doesn't have any ornaments apart from a string of pearls, her exquisite face definitely draws the attention of all men in the room.

"Oh, do forgive me for arriving late," she says breathlessly, coming toward us. "Our carriage broke down on the road, and it took such a long time for our coachman to ride to the nearest village for help."

"What an unfortunate incident!" Philip says. "Is anyone injured? I'll call our doctor."

"Father has a scratch on his leg, but it's nothing to cause great worry over." She sees me; for a second her eyes narrow, but then she breaks into a radiant smile and holds out her hand. "My name is Lillie; I am Constance's sister. Are you the famous Lady Katriona who has captured Edward's heart?" She says Edward's name in a casual tone that hints they are well acquainted.

"Pleased to meet you," I say. "I'm Kat—I mean, you can call me Kat."

"Lillie will be coming out next year." There's a note of pride in Constance's tone. "If her mother cannot make the journey, I will be accompanying her to court."

Lillie's smile wavers for a second. She darts a glance at Edward. "If Mama wasn't so determined to perfect my wardrobe, I could have had my season this year."

There's no doubt that she deeply regrets the delay. What difference does not debuting this year make? A seed of suspicion starts to form in my mind.

Lillie turns to Edward. "Guess what? I've brought you several tulip bulbs from Enrilth. If we try cultivating them in the palace now, they'll be a treat for next year's flower show."

I blink. I didn't expect her to be into gardening.

"I appreciate the gesture," Edward says. "But I'd rather leave the credit to you."

"Edward, I bought them especially for you." Lillie's tone is plaintive—a bit whiny even. "I trust your skills will do them better justice than mine. You've never refused me before."

"Lillie," Constance says in a low, urgent voice, giving me a lightning glance.

It's official: she's the 999th girl to have a crush on Edward.

❧ 10 ❧

The journey was so tiring that I slept until midmorning the next day, so Constance had Amelie bring me a late breakfast tray instead. Then she took me on a tour of the house, which lasted so long that we were late for lunch. I counted two grand halls, three dining rooms, four parlors, and a dozen sitting rooms. There's a healer's room for the family doctor, as Constance boasts that they don't need to ride to the nearest town for medical-related emergencies. They even have special rooms including a lamp room, a china room, and a muniment room where they keep parochial records, charters, deeds, and other important documents. Bedrooms are too many to count, and there's even a "bachelor's row" to separate the single guests from the married. The steward and butler and housekeeper get their own rooms, while the rest of the servants share a servants' hall that reminds me of a hostel or dormitory. Even though the duke's house lacks a throne room and palace guards and other stuff that comes with the royal package, it is pretty overwhelming. Constance seems pleased whenever my jaw drops or I let out a gasp.

Edward has gone grouse-shooting with the men—a popular

pastime with the titled and wealthy, so I am left with the women. Everyone is nauseatingly polite and respectful, even when I occasionally behave like a country bumpkin, which again reminds me of how they ignored me in the past. I'm sure few of the smiles they give me are sincere, and it bothers me that I have to paste a huge, fake smile on my face in return. Again, I wish Poppy or Elle were here with me.

At noon, when the men return with cartloads of game from the shooting, Constance insists on having a picnic outside since the weather is uncommonly warm today. Like a general barking orders to soldiers, she directs the servants to set up a buffet style table on the lawn, with clusters of small round tables under the trees. As I observe her discussing with the butler the choices of meat and the seating arrangements, I realize this is the kind of woman that Madame Dubois wants me to emulate. Organized, efficient, well acquainted with every single minute detail and rule. Which is so not me.

The table looks in danger of crashing from the weight of food placed on it. There are platters of pheasants and partridges and deer, a giant wooden bowl of salad greens, slabs of cheese and fresh rye bread, cakes and jellies and puddings, and coffee and tea. I don't even know where to start.

I look for Edward, but he is already occupied with Philip, Henry, and other men. I suppose it isn't appropriate that we stick together like glue all the time, so I quash the awkward, shy part of me that's threatening to rear, and do my best to socialize. Even though I'd rather sit away from the crowd with a book.

"Where are the children?" I ask, looking around. I remember Rosie smiling shyly at me, and I wouldn't mind seeing her again.

Constance looks surprised. "In the nursery, of course. It is the governess's responsibility to take care of them."

The tone of her voice suggests that I had said something

foolish. Excuse me, but neither my lady nor princess lessons has covered anything concerning children. "Um, I just thought since the weather is so nice today, they might enjoy having lunch outside with us."

"Children have no business mixing up with the grown-ups," Lady Fremont says coldly. She's been civil enough, but there's something in her eyes that sparks of resentment. Which is perfectly understandable. Her two prospects for her daughter— Edward and Henry—have been snapped up by me and Elle. "They will have plenty of time for social activities in a few years."

Constance digs a fork into her watercress salad. "God knows that I wish they never grow up. It really makes one feel old, you know. I know I shall resent it when the time comes for Rosie to be brought out."

"How is Rosie getting along recently?" Lady Mansfield asks. She also treated me like I never existed, especially since I ruined her dinner party by splashing champagne on Andrew McVean, but now she can't be more friendly. "Didn't you tell us that your eldest tried to lead her astray?"

"She has much improved now, thank heaven." Constance rubs her forehead as though to ward off a headache. "Tristan has always spoiled her dreadfully, but taking her to the woods to go climbing trees, jumping over stiles, and getting her frock dirty and torn? I had to put my foot down. I could not have my little girl growing up a savage."

"You won't have cause for worry, since most of the time the boys are away at boarding school."

"Well, that reminds me. I need to give Tristan another talk when he comes back. He may have stopped with shaping her into a tomboy, but he's been feeding Rosie's head with ideas lately."

"What kind of ideas?"

Constance presses her lips in a slash. "He calls them

modern, but I call them dreadful. He lent Rosie his books at that boarding school—books that a pure-minded young girl shouldn't be around. I confiscated one book that had pictures of the human anatomy. It is positively disgraceful for her to be learning about such distasteful stuff when she should be concentrating on her own lessons. I told her to put everything she read out of her mind and worry about performing a court curtsy."

"You needn't worry, Constance," Lady Fremont says, simpering. "Considering that Rosie is your daughter, and a little beauty who takes after her mother, she won't have much trouble with suitors."

"Making the right choice for marriage is no easy deal," Lady Petunia says, joining the conversation. "You don't know how much I have pleaded with Henry to pick a suitable girl from a good family, but he has been fixated on that Bradshaw girl. She might no longer be a servant, but the fact remains that she lacks a lady's education. Did you know that she offered to help me do my hair? As if I didn't have enough maids for that."

She sends me an irritated glance. As if I had anything to do with getting Henry and Elle together. If anything, my original goal was to separate them so Elle could marry Edward. But with so many women present, I'm worried that any defense of Elle might backfire and produce an opposite effect. From how Constance seemed so concerned about making Rosie into a little lady, I doubt any of them will approve of a union between Henry and Elle. Heck, I'm pretty sure that they don't think too highly of me either—a girl who tripped over her feet during her presentation.

"Excuse me," I murmur and get up. The aroma of roast pheasant is assailing my nose, and my mouth is watering after pretending to be satisfied with a meager plate of salad. Plus, I need a break from the conversation—it's getting more and more difficult to smile and agree with their views.

I grab a plate and help myself liberally to food. Even in the palace, you can't get pheasant that's caught on the same day it's cooked. Let Constance and the others gape at my appetite; I have endured their conversation all morning and I'll be pissed off if I need to endure an empty stomach as well.

Laughter rings out near me, just when I poured myself a tall glass of lemonade to go with my piled plate. Then someone stumbles in my back, my hand is jolted, and a chunk of meat falls on my dress. Half of my lemonade spills down my front.

"Oh I'm so sorry!" Lillie gasps. "I was talking to Mother and didn't notice you behind me."

Her mother also apologizes profusely, but like Lady Fremont, I sense the same restrained resentment in her face. Unless I'm much mistaken, Lillie's mother also harbors anger toward me—anger that I stole her daughter's chance to be queen.

I tell myself to stop speculating; for all I know, they could be genuinely upset about humiliating me in front of the party.

"It's all right, don't worry about it." I squat on the grass to pick up the meat off the ground. A small gasp comes from Lillie; immediately a servant rushes over and tells me not to trouble myself.

"Katriona . . ."

"I'm fine. Just excuse me for a moment."

I slip away from the picnic buffet, dabbing my soaked front with a handkerchief. Actually I'm not too miffed about Lillie, since her accident gives me a perfect chance to get away from the crowd. I feel the need to breathe in privacy after all the socializing since breakfast.

Amelie doesn't say anything when she learns what's happened. There's a peeved look on her face as she strips me down, tosses away the soiled dress, and laces me into a new gown. But when she finishes tying on my sash, she puts her hands on her hips.

"Don't you think it's an accident, Princess. That younger sister of Constance Maynard has been hankering after His Highness since her sister married Duke Philip."

"I don't think she could cause anything to come between Edward and me." Judging from the age of Constance's children, she must have married more than a decade ago. If Lillie knew Edward that early, he would have chosen her way before we met.

"I'm not saying that His Highness will change his affections, he's hopeless. But what I'm saying is that you ought take a firmer stance. Make it clear that you won't stand for any insult. You're the princess."

"So what do you suggest I should have done?" I ask, curious but also amused. "Pour the remaining lemonade in my glass over her dress?

A rare smile appears on her face. Amelie really looks prettier when she smiles. I wish she'd smile more often.

"Well, no," she admits. "But while you've got a spirit when it comes to injustice, you're not strong enough when dealing with those girls with the mind of a shark. You could have made her take responsibility for ruining your dress or warn her to be more careful the next time."

I nod, remembering how Lillie gazes longingly at Edward whenever he isn't looking in her direction. "If there is a next time."

On my way back, I hear a little cry of pain. Under a large tree lies a girl in a crumpled heap. It's the same girl who shrieked like the world's end is coming when Krev let loose a mouse in the ball.

"You there," she calls to a passing servant. "I tripped over a root and I think I sprained my ankle."

"Certainly, miss," the servant says anxiously. "I'll fetch the family doctor for you."

"No!" She exclaims in a vehement tone. "Go and find Henry

—the duke of Somerset. It's just a minor sprain, he will be able to see to it."

"But we have a doctor on the premises . . ."

"Which part of my request escapes your understanding?" she says icily. "Now go!"

Is she trying to get Henry's attention? Since Edward is already taken, it's possible that Henry looks a lot more attractive at the moment. My gaze falls on a rose bush nearby, and an evil idea enters my head.

I stalk to the bush, pick up a twig lying on the grass, and hook a fat caterpillar onto the twig. I return to the girl, pretend that I'm just passing by, and tell her I'd go for a doctor.

"Oh, please don't trouble yourself, Lady Katriona," she says, flustered. Her attitude has changed completely from bossy to fawning. "I have already sent a servant."

"Very well." I drop the twig and the caterpillar lands on her dress. It wriggles for a second and starts to crawl.

"Eek!"

She lets out a shriek and leaps into the air—so high that I'm sure she broke her own record at the ball. Much to my amusement, she scrambles up and runs off with no sign of any injury. Her shrieks can still be heard even when she's out of sight.

Muffled laughter reaches my ears. I look for the source and find Edward striding towards me, his shoulders shaking as he tries to suppress his laughter.

"What?"

"You . . . never fail to amaze me, Kat," he says, his shoulders still shaking.

"I didn't even have time to apologize to her when she took off running." I grin sheepishly. "This Little Season thing really is as exaggerated as you described. By the way, how come you're here?"

"I was concerned when you disappeared." He gives me that intense gaze that I have become familiar with. "I told myself that you're strong enough, that you wouldn't care about the stupid mishap, but in the end I had to come and find you. And I find that not only are you completely unaffected, but you also scared off a scheming girl? Life is never dull when you're in it."

In the back of my mind, a voice whispers that this life isn't going to last, but I push it down.

"I'm glad you came to get me," I say, and I mean it. "It's only half a day that we have been apart, and already I missed you. I wanted to come and sit with you, but you are with the men and I didn't want to appear too needy . . ."

"I was thinking exactly the same thing. So what do you say that we steal away for some time alone?"

"I'd love to," I say without thinking, and he smiles. "But won't the others be concerned if we don't show up?"

"The picnic is almost over and some have already retired to their rooms. Come," he says, grasping my hand and leading me away. "There's something I want to show you."

Fallen leaves crunch under our feet as we make our way to the front of the house. There, surrounded by slender young fir trees, is the lake—smooth, glittering, and crystal clear.

Edward strides toward a small rowing boat and starts unwinding the rope that tethers the boat to shore. I quicken my pace, intending to help him, but the boat is already free by the time I reach him.

He turns to me and holds out his hand, his eyes glowing with heart-melting warmth. "I always like to come for a row whenever I visit Cousin Philip."

I step carefully in the boat, careful not to let my long skirts catch around my shoes. Edward helps me before he steps in himself, then he takes the oars and we glide away on the mirror-like lake. The water laps quietly against the boat, and fresh air cools my skin, making me feel refreshed and peaceful and just . . . happy.

"I wish we could have a trip of our own," I blurt. "Just for the two of us, without loads of people hanging around."

Edward lets out a sigh, his expression regretful. "There is nothing else that I'd rather do, but we have been uncommonly busy lately, and I'm afraid that taking a trip for pleasure may reflect negatively on our family. Industrialization has solved many problems in this country, but it has also brought a new set of problems—as you are also well aware. There is much to deal with."

Disappointment is evident in his tone. I reach out and squeeze his hand. "It's all right," I say softly. "There is still your garden. And the closet in the hallway."

His mouth quirks up with amusement.

"Let us wait until after our engagement; perhaps the work-load will lessen after my father and I review the reports from Parliament." His eyes grow dreamy as he stares at the surrounding scenery. "I would like to show you Enrilth, the village where I grew up. It is not as glamorous as Northport, but I'm sure you would like it better."

I nod and smile. Hopefully this dream of our own getaway will be realized one day.

There's a tiny pop, and an ugly, pointed-eared creature appears, hanging a few feet above Edward's head.

It's Krev.

❧ 11 ❧

Krev has followed me to Northport? Since I entered the palace, I've tried calling to him a couple times, but he never responded. Not that he paid much heed even when I kept yelling for him to help me get out of Athelia. Still, I'd expect him to check up on me sometimes. It seemed that once Edward chose me at the ball, Krev considered his mission done and wouldn't have anything more to do with me. Then what is he doing here?

"Kat?" Edward looks concerned. "Is there something wrong?"

I rub my eyes. But there's nothing in the air now—did I just imagine the goblin appearing, or did Krev suddenly disappear again?

"I . . . I thought I saw . . ." I shake my head. "Never mind."

THE RITZ. THAT'S WHAT I FIRST THINK OF WHEN I ENTER THE room Constance has arranged for me. It's large and luxurious, just like everything in the house. The bed has a heavy crimson canopy embroidered in gold, the carpets look like Oriental imports, and everything else is done in a white-and-gold theme —cream and chintz and glass.

But it's the view that really gets me. When Amelie pulls the curtains apart, there's a grand view of the lake outside. I can see how the wind stirs up the glittering waters and the trees surround the lake like guardians. When I sit on the velvet-draped chair and stare outside, I can almost believe myself some wealthy person on a weekend trip. The roses that I received earlier are now placed in a crystal vase on a small table near the window. I wish I could share my room with Edward. But of course, since we aren't even officially engaged, there's no way he can stay with me.

At night, I draw up the blankets to my chin. I wish I had a novel to read before falling asleep, but there isn't any sign of a book. Constance is a great hostess, but apparently, books are not kept in bedrooms.

I am dozing off to sleep when there's a pop and a flash of light. An ugly goblin hovers in the air, his pointy ears brushing the top of the canopy.

"Krev!" I sit up immediately. "Is that really you? Was that you at the lake? Why did you disappear?"

He grins, baring a row of pointy teeth. "You were with Eddie so I had to wait until you were alone. I couldn't very well make you talk to me when I'm invisible to Eddie."

"Where have you been? I've called out to you a couple of times, but you never appeared."

He flips upside down, his legs sticking up toward the ceiling.

"Morag gave birth to a baby daughter, and we've been having a huge celebration. Besides, you're going to marry Eddie anyway, so there's nothing to bet on. When's the wedding —tomorrow?"

"Of course not." I don't say it, but of course I can't bear to leave Edward so soon. "We aren't even engaged yet."

Krev flies a bit closer. "But you two *are* getting married, aren't you?"

"You're getting concerned for the happy ending?"

"Well, Barthelius just wanted to make sure that the old Katriona is able to return."

I feel as though he doused me with a bucket of ice-cold water. "You . . . you mean that when I leave, she will come back into this body?"

"You can't expect Eddie to stay unmarried for his entire life, can you? Eventually, she'll have to return. It's only a question of when it'll happen."

I could punch him. "Do you mean to say that all my efforts have been for nothing? I mean, if I don't do anything, the happy ending will occur anyway?"

Krev has the grace to look guilty. "Look, Eddie is a little picky—"

"That's an understatement."

"—but there are thousands and thousands of eligible girls in Athelia. Even if he doesn't fall in love with Elle, he will find a girl someday. It could take years, but he's the heir to the throne —do you honestly expect he'd never marry?"

Anger surges in my chest. I clench my hands to prevent myself from hitting him. "If that's the case, why did you keep egging me on? Why did you have to tell me I had to finish the story?"

The goblin shrugs. "Too much fun watching you struggle."

My fist connects with his nose. Krev lands on the bed with a yelp. I would have followed up with another punch, but a huge wave of fear, worry, and dread crashes over me. I sink back to the bed, unable to repress the tears forming in my eyes.

Krev regains his equilibrium; he bounces up, snarling, but freezes when a tear runs down my cheek.

"Girlie, what's there to cry about? You've been through some rough patches, but you got to the happy ending. Wasn't that what you wanted all along—to go back to the human world?"

I swipe my sleeve over my eyes.

"Krev . . . this Story World . . . is it only a dream I'm living in? Edward, and everyone else . . . they're fictional characters, right? They aren't *real*, are they? They just feel real because I'm in the book."

Krev looks waspish. "What do you want me to say?"

"The truth." *Even if it's going to break my heart.*

He props a hand under his chin. "Don't go bawling again. Your eyes will show it in the morning." Then he blows air out of his cheeks and shakes his head. "My, you have fallen really hard for Eddie."

I don't say anything. I just stare at him. Before the ball, I was way too occupied with achieving the happy ending to ask more questions, but now I need to know more.

"The magic Barthelius weaved into the book is a highly complex spell," Krev begins. "He was super powerful a hundred years ago—in fact, he's what you humans call a child genius. He didn't just create the book you held—he created a whole alternative realm. It's supposed to be closed off to humans unless they tamper with the book. You entered Athelia through a portal that was produced in the cover you ripped off."

My breath catches in my throat. *This is insane.* "But . . . if Athelia was created a hundred years ago, was it still in existence when I ripped the book?"

"Of course. It has continued to exist even after the original happily-ever-after ending. Since you damaged the book, a time-turning spell was triggered, taking you right to the beginning."

"Wait . . . did you mention an original happy ending? Does that mean Edward did marry Elle after all? How could it happen?"

Krev rolls his eyes. "Dunno. We'll never find out since you

have altered Athelia's history. Now, the records are going to say that Edward married the second daughter of Earl Bradshaw."

His words weigh heavily on me like a sack of potatoes pressing me down. If only I hadn't tried to help Elle get together with Edward. If I'd just relaxed and waited for Edward to eventually fall in love and marry, I wouldn't have meddled with Athelia's history. But it's too late. Katriona is going to come back—as the princess.

"What is Katriona like?"

"Haven't a clue." Krev sounds annoyed. "Didn't you listen to me? The book occurred a hundred years ago. Barthelius doesn't even remember who the fairy godmother is. Look, if you're that concerned about Eddie, why don't you find another bride for him? Then he won't have to deal with the real Katriona."

I feel like punching him again. "How could you make such a callous suggestion, after everything that we've been through? He isn't a puppet for me to manipulate. He's a human being."

Krev doesn't seem affected. Not surprising, since he was cruel enough to advise that Edward ditch me and find another, as though he could switch his feelings on and off. I honestly believe that the goblins don't know what the word 'feeling' means.

"Don't be so sensitive, girlie. Eddie knew what he was getting into when he decided to marry you. Besides, who said you have to take my suggestion? You've always told me my ideas are crap anyway."

I throw my pillow at him. "Get out."

When he disappears, I let the tears flow for a moment, until I realize that my crying will reflect in my eyes the next morning. I force myself to swallow the lump in my throat and go to sleep. But even though I've successfully repressed the tears, I can't repress the pain that's growing in my heart.

In the morning, Amelie enters my room to help me dress. I stare blankly at the mirror, a hollow feeling in my chest. When I think of Edward being stuck with the old Katriona, no matter what she is really like, I feel as if my heart is breaking.

"You look awfully serious," Amelie commented, running a brush through my hair. "Are you worried about His Highness?"

How does she know? Only Edward knows the truth. And Poppy, though she remains skeptical.

"Don't worry," Amelie says briskly. "Lillie Maynard may be scheming to get His Highness, but he will watch out for himself. And even if she does succeed in getting him into a compromising position, he would never agree to marry her. Especially when he announced his choice at the ball."

Lillie. It's obvious that she is head-over-heels in love with Edward. I hate to say this, but I admit I'm jealous. Not just because she's hot enough to be an A-list actress, but also because of the gardening knowledge she shares with Edward. I can't get a word into their conversation whenever she comes to talk to him. Although Edward did teach me how to recognize and tend to certain flowers, I can never match his passion for nature.

Suddenly, Krev's suggestion about Edward finding another girl—however undesirable it sounds—enters my head. I don't know anything about the old Katriona, but might it not be a better option if someone like Lillie takes my place when I'm gone? Lillie might not be mature enough in her way of treating me, but compared to the other girls, she is the best candidate for Edward. She'd be a better princess for Athelia. I shiver for a second. I feel as though I'm making a will.

"But everyone knows that Edward and I are to be engaged."

"Doesn't mean that she won't try something devious." Amelie shrugs. "But like I said, you don't have anything to worry about. His Highness will guard himself well."

I picture Lillie with Edward. They'd make a gorgeous

couple, even though my heart screams against getting them together. And if the old Katriona is anything like Bianca . . .

No. I don't want that to happen. I don't want someone like Bianca to get him. Bianca only wants him because he never noticed her.

"Your Highness?" There's a note of alarm in Amelie's voice now. I decide it's best to change the subject.

"By the way, what do you think about Bertram? I mean, he has a crush on you . . ."

"What's a crush?"

"Oh, sorry. I meant that he seems to really like you, and I just wanted to know if you could give him a chance."

Amelie catches a wayward curl and pins it to the back of my head. I wonder if she prefers not to answer my question, until she finally speaks.

"To tell the truth, I don't really plan on marrying."

Now this is shocking. Very few Athelian women—whether they are noble or common-born—would declare a life of celibacy.

"Why not?"

"My sister suffered from a horrible marriage for ten years. Her scum of a husband didn't work, gambled away her earnings, and hit her in broad daylight, just because she didn't cook the fish to his liking!" Amelie takes a deep breath. "It took another three years for us to help her obtain a divorce. Father had to put a mortgage on the house."

"You can get divorced in Athelia?"

"Easier for those who can afford to hire a lawyer. I've heard that a third of the nobles got divorced."

A third! Maybe it shouldn't be that surprising, since marriages among the rich and powerful are rarely based on love. From my experience in the Season, a lot of men and women meet for a few times and then the man proposes.

I wonder what the odds are of the prince getting a divorce if the real Katriona doesn't get along with him.

Hang on, we're talking about Bertram here. I have to put in a good word for him, even if Amelie seems determined to stay single.

"Come on, surely you don't believe Bertram will treat you that badly? Even if he looks kind of scary when he doesn't smile, he wouldn't dare lay a finger on you. Actually, if anyone were to ask me, I'd say *you* are more intimidating than him."

"My sister's husband was as meek as a lamb when she first met him." Amelie lays down the brush with a decisive thud. "All I want to do now is to keep my job and lead a peaceful life."

Poor Bertram.

❧ 12 ❧

"So, what did you do to attract His Highness?"

Dozens of beautifully powdered faces stare at me. I'm sitting with the noble ladies while Edward is again grouse-hunting with the men. I would have liked to have gone with them, but Edward told me that although there was no rule preventing women from joining a shooting party, it would look especially awkward if I were the only woman who wanted to go out and watch men firing at pheasants and geese and ducks. And so, I have to stay indoors with the ladies, who have nothing better to do except to talk, sip tea, and play cards.

"We have been *dying* to learn how you seduced the prince," Claire says, her eyes brimming with curiosity. I can almost imagine her thrusting a mic beneath my chin like a reporter.

"Um . . ." I reach for the teacup only to find it already empty.

"Pardon my bluntness, but Bianca usually attracts more attention. Fancy sharing with us how you managed to capture our prince's heart?"

I really wish I could escape from this room. "I . . . I kind of met him when I went to see Elle and her mother."

"Do you mean the servant girl who turned out to be the daughter of the late earl?" Constance says. "Such a fascinating story! I've been looking forward to meeting her, but unfortunately she is too busy to come."

The conversation turns to Elle and the amazing story of how she elevated her status from penniless servant to daughter of an earl. Perhaps it's just as well that Lady Petunia had a headache this morning, most likely from drinking too much wine the previous night, or she'd be irritated that so many women are intrigued by Elle. However, while Constance is fascinated by Elle's rags-to-riches story, I don't think she'd be happy to welcome Elle as a daughter-in-law. Seeing that I'm unwilling to talk too much about Edward, the ladies gradually let their attention move toward other juicy bits. I hear about Lord Alfred writing letters to Lady Bracknell—who is already married, by the way—and how Lady Priscilla has produced five daughters—too bad she has failed to produce a son—and that Minnie May is coming out soon, and would someone please draw up a list of eligible suitors for her?

It's all so very boring, so I keep drinking cup after cup, even though I'm not a huge fan of chamomile tea, until I actually have to leave for the toilet. Athelia does have toilets that flush; however, only the richest can afford them—just as with cameras. Some modern appliances exist, though they're still in the early stages. In fact, Edward has mentioned to me that they are building a new railroad, which will be completed by the time of the wedding.

"Excuse me," I say, rising. "I need to be gone for a moment. I'm afraid I had too much tea."

On my way out, I run into Lillie. She has her hair down, and it curls gently on her shoulders. A perfect, angelic beauty.

"Hello." I give her a smile. I would keep going if she didn't call my name.

"May I speak to you for a moment?"

"Um . . ." The bathroom is just around the corner. "All right."

Lillie clasps her hands together. "I . . . I would like to apologize to you."

"Whatever for?"

She looks up at me hesitantly. "Constance said I appeared rather *forward* with Edward. So, I wished to seek you and explain."

I debate whether I should mention to her that there was this girl who sent Edward a baleful letter, dotted with tear stains, asking him why he didn't choose her at the ball. Or the other amazingly resourceful girl who managed to ambush him when he was going to the greenhouse—Bertram caught that one before she could get Edward into a compromising situation. Neither girl, of course, had bothered explaining anything to me.

"I've known Edward since Constance married his cousin," Lillie says, smoothing back a lock of her hair. "I wasn't much older than Rosie, but he was so kind and attentive to me. I had my own garden at home, and he was instrumental in helping me choose the seeds and species. I've rarely interacted with anyone outside family, since I haven't been brought out, so Edward has become my best friend."

What am I supposed to say? *Thanks for telling me; now, get lost.*

"Will you forgive me, Katriona?" Lillie says, her tone plaintive. "I really hope that I didn't cause any misunderstanding between you."

"You didn't." Edward didn't even mention a word about Lillie. Not that we have managed to talk much in private, especially amid a house party. "Now, if you'll excuse me—my bladder is going to burst."

Her eyes widen in shock. I don't know if it's because the word "bladder" is rarely used or if she's realized she's been keeping me too long, but I don't bother to find out. Nature calls —an emergency call, in fact.

When I emerge from the bathroom, I notice in the mirror that one of my hairpins has fallen out, and my hair is in danger of breaking free. I decide to head back to my room.

Somehow, I get lost. This Pemberley-like place isn't as enormous as the palace, but I've only been here for a day. And I have never been good at directions. I used to get lost in my own school even after one semester.

I hurry along the corridor and find myself on a balcony. It's not the typical kind that projects outside a building, but rather, it overlooks a larger room on the lower level. Rosie is bent over a desk, her face screwed up in concentration as she writes in a book.

It is rather interesting to observe her from where I stand. I suspect that the construction of this balcony is quite convenient for the parents wanting to check up on their children. After all, no one has surveillance cameras in Athelia.

And then I hear a door being thrown open, and Thomas swaggers into the room. He slams a fist on her desk.

"Roly-poly! Have you stolen Tristan's old stuff again?"

Rosie quickly slips the book into the desk. "I don't know what you're talking about."

"I've been looking for his arithmetic workbook, volume two. Come—hand it over. I know you sneaked it from Tristan's room when I was away in boarding school."

He stalks over to her, his hand outstretched. Rosie's lip quivers, but she shakes her head. "You can get away with copying the answers, but you'd still flunk the tests. And then you'll get in worse trouble when Father gets your report card."

I can't see Thomas's face, but I'm pretty sure he's mad. "Don't you play Goody Two-shoes with me, Little Miss Rosie. It's not like those workbooks are going to do you any good.

Girls have no business doing arithmetic anyway. Your brain isn't fit for mental exertion."

Now, that's going too far. I take the staircase that leads to the lower level and easily find the room where Rosie and Thomas are speaking. I fling the door wide open. "Morning." I offer what I hope is a charming smile. "Sorry for barging in without knocking, but I heard you talking about arithmetic and wondered if I could be of some help."

Rosie stares at me, her eyes round and wide, her delicate white hands gripping the sides of her desk.

Thomas looks as though he just swallowed a live fish. "What did you just say?"

"You heard me, but I guess you didn't understand. So allow me repeat it: I could help you with your math—arithmetic—problems." I keep my smile confident and push down any bit of doubt I'm having. Math was never my strong suit, but I'm pretty sure my high school math skills are sufficient for the problems in a thirteen-year-old's arithmetic workbook. Plus, if he needed to copy the answers from his older brother's book, he can't be too bright.

"Ladies don't mess with academics." Thomas doesn't look at me, but his voice is gruff. He doesn't treat me with the same harsh condescension he has shown toward his sister, but it's only because I'm a princess.

"This one does." I put my hands on my hips. Maybe I shouldn't interfere with their education —after all, this is nothing like child labor—but Thomas's disparaging remark about a girl's mental capability has gotten on my nerves. I don't want Rosie believing that she's inferior.

"How about a bet? Suppose you show me your arithmetic workbook, and I'll work on the problems you want to copy from Tristan's. Rosie has the old workbook with answers, so we can compare to see if mine are correct. If there's a single question that I can't do, then I'll ask Bertram to take you riding."

From an earlier conversation with Constance, I know that Thomas is obsessed with horses, and Bertram is a great trainer. As I expected, the boy's face lights up. "But if I *can* complete every problem, then you'll promise not to bother Rosie. You will apologize and concede that a girl is capable of studying the same subjects as a boy."

Both children seem taken aback at my confidence.

"Aunt Kat," Rosie says hesitantly. "Have you taken arithmetic lessons before?"

I just give her an enigmatic smile. "What do you say, Thomas? Or are you so terrified of losing that you don't even want to bet?"

That does the trick. "Fine." Thomas plunks his workbook—which looks brand-new—on Rosie's desk.

🐿 I 3 🐿

The men caught an avalanche of birds from their hunt. For breakfast, we have roast pheasant, partridge, chicken sandwiches with buttered cucumbers, and turkey meatballs dipped in a rich tomato-and-cheese sauce. There's more than enough to feed an army, which makes me cringe. Back home, I remember how Mom would save scraps or freeze leftovers for us whenever she wasn't going to be available. Anything home-cooked was better than pizza and burgers.

I mention to Constance about the abundance of food, but she just pats my arm. "Don't worry, dear—I always arrange for the leftovers to be packed into food baskets. We will be going over to the village to distribute the food." She smiles. "Part of our duty, you see."

An image of those villagers lining up to welcome Edward and me pops up in my mind. Serfdom—that's what Philip and Constance are running here. Maybe it's normal, and maybe the villagers are happy with the arrangement. Still, it doesn't mean I should be comfortable with it. I take up my fork, making a deliberate decision to finish everything on my plate.

When Edward takes his seat across from me, I smile at him.

Yesterday, I had a total victory over Thomas. I did have some apprehension about completing the questions, but it turns out I needn't have worried. My high school math totally trumped his thirteen-year-old Athelia-boarding-school math.

Edward smiles back, but there is a questioning look in his eyes as though he's wondering why I'm in a good mood this early in the morning. Usually, I'm grumpy and impatient—at the palace, I rarely get much sleep because of the onerous and time-consuming princess duties. I start to open my mouth, but Lillie glides into the room, radiant as usual, and pauses near us.

"May I sit here?"

While Constance imposes formality with dinners, even going as far as installing name cards on the table, she's more lax when it comes to breakfast. Since everyone gets up at different times in the morning, there is less restriction on where people can sit. Lillie doesn't really have to ask, but she glances at me as though she needs my validation.

Back off; he's mine.

"Go ahead." I shrug.

She looks as if I just tossed her a piece of candy. A servant pulls out her chair, and she sits down, a smile playing on her lips as she shakes out a napkin and spreads it on her lap.

"Did you know that we are going to the village today?" Her eyes follow Edward's.

Edward nods and takes up his cup. "You will also be going, I presume?"

"Of course. Will you please take me to the gardening store? I would love to have some advice on how to plot my own garden."

A stab of jealousy hits me, but I resolve not to let it show. I remember what Krev said about the old Katriona coming back, and I tell myself that Lillie is a better replacement. There are still eight months—longer than the time that Edward and I have known each other. And even if my marriage to Edward cannot be nulled, he will be able to divorce the old Katriona and marry Lillie instead. Amelie had said that divorces aren't that uncommon for nobles.

"I thought you already had your own garden." There's a hint of frost in Edward's tone.

"It needs to be redesigned. And I would dearly appreciate if you could help me with it."

Claire, who is sitting next to me, starts to ask questions about my new life in the palace. How do I feel now I'm princess? When is the engagement going to take place? Have I picked my gown for the ceremony? They're tedious questions, but they keep my attention away from Edward and Lillie. Edward looks at me now and then, but I harden my heart and force myself to keep talking to Claire.

Let him go, Kat. He deserves better.

When breakfast is over, Edward comes up to me.

"I am afraid that we won't be able to share a carriage," he says, touching my arm. "There is a shortage of carriages, so you will have to sit with the other women. I will go on horse."

"Um . . . do you mind if I choose not to go? I promised Rosie I would spend the day with her."

He raises his eyebrows. "Since when do you know her so well?"

I brief him on the little drama I had yesterday with Thomas and Rosie. "You see, after I made Thomas eat his words, Rosie looked at me like I was some kind of hero. She doesn't have much company apart from a simple-minded governess, so I told her I'd go to her."

"Then I shall stay with you. Let me inform Constance that there is a change of plans."

"But you promised, Edward," Lillie says, suddenly appearing next to him. "You promised that you would help me select my catalogue."

"It's all right," I quickly say. "Really, there's no need for you to stay as well. Constance will be disappointed if both of us choose to remain behind when she has already arranged for us to go. And Lillie needs your help just as Rosie needs mine."

Edward fixes his gaze on me—piercing, shrewd, probing. There's a flash of hurt as well; it disappears as quickly as a shooting star. I stare back unflinchingly. *The old Katriona is coming back*, I chant in my head. *Lillie will be a better choice.*

"Don't worry about me. I'll be fine with Rosie."

"Very well." His voice is calm, but when he walks past me, he leans over for a second, and his lips brush past my ear. "You may try, but you will not succeed."

Before I can respond, he is already heading toward the door that leads to the parlor. Lillie throws me a smirk—I get the impression she is pleased that Edward has decided to go ahead without me. For a moment, I itch to pull her away, grab Edward's arm, and say I'm sorry. But I don't want him spending the rest of his life with the old Katriona—a girl I'm sure he barely knows. A girl who could be similar to Bianca.

I bite my lip and wait till Edward and Lillie have disappeared from sight.

⚜

ROSIE IS DOING NEEDLEWORK WHEN I ARRIVE. HER HEAD IS bent over a snowy white dress, her pale blond curls spilling over her shoulder, the thimble on her thumb gleaming silver as she sits by the window. From a distance, she looks like the ideal Athelian woman—demure, patient, hardworking. But as I approach her, the dress on her lap seems too large and cumbersome. Moreover, despite being of similar age, her face lacks Paige's carefree, bucolic expression.

"Hello, Rosie."

Her hand pauses and she looks up. Her entire face lights up. "Aunt Kat! You really came!"

"It's Kat," I say, leaning over her chair. "Don't you have a maid or a servant to sew for you?" Not that there's anything wrong with Rosie doing her own work, but after witnessing the army Constance commands, it feels strange to me that she can't just get someone else to do menial tasks.

She shrugs. "Mama said *every* girl must learn how to use a needle and thread. Sometimes Thomas makes me sew the buttons on his shirt even though he can have Faith do it."

Yeah, Thomas does look capable of bullying his little sister. Still, I'm surprised that she has to do embroidery when she's only nine.

"Isn't it the same with you, Kat?" Rosie's large eyes are full of curiosity. "Don't you have to do things for your father—and brothers, if you have any?"

"My father passed away when I was a child. And no, I don't have any brothers." *One Bianca is enough*, I mutter in my head. "But surely you have other stuff you can learn. That math book your older brother gave you . . . do you have math lessons?"

Rosie shakes her head and looks down. "Mama said a girl ought to learn music and literature to the extent of making her company pleasant with a male acquaintance."

"Rubbish," I say without thinking. Her mouth falls open; she stares at me—an altogether familiar expression for those moments when I let slip evidence of my un-Athelian upbringing. I really should conceal it when I can, but sometimes there are things—such as child labor—that are too shocking for me to keep my mouth zipped. "You only need to learn for yourself. And I don't get why you don't need to learn math." I remember Poppy, her brow furrowed as she tried to balance the checkbook while Elle explained patiently to her. "Look, you're supposed to grow up and get married and run a household, right? What if you give a servant some money for purchases, and he comes back with the wrong change, and you couldn't tell the difference? Do you want to be swindled?"

Rosie is speechless.

"Um . . ." I drop my hand when I realize I've been waving in the air. "Sorry. But I just thought you should know. Don't mind me."

"But Papa said that girls can't think for themselves, and that's what men are for."

I try very hard not to roll my eyes. No wonder Thomas acted so condescending. "But what about Tristan? Didn't he give you his workbook?"

"Papa said he always had weird ideas. That's why he told me that I should keep the book out of sight."

"Do *you* want to study it? Don't give me any more of that 'Papa said' or 'Mama said' stuff. Tell me what you really think."

Rosie glances at me, still kind of bemused, but I give her a firm nod. "Tell me."

"I . . . I guess I don't want to be stupid," she says, her hand bunching around a handful of the dress. "That's what Thomas always calls me."

I pull up a chair. "Great. I'm glad you said that."

We spend the next hour or so plowing through Tristan's workbook. Rosie had to dig up an even older one because the one Thomas wanted to copy was too advanced. I show her how to add and subtract, and how to recite the multiplication table. She is a bit slow in the beginning, but after working through the same sum over and over again, she seems to grasp the concept, and the rest of the problems go much quicker.

While Rosie works at her desk, I walk around the room. There are dolls sitting in a cushioned chair, a bright, painted rocking horse in a corner, and a couple of rubber balls. Of course, I can't resist browsing the bookshelf. Books with titles like "*How to Be a Good Daughter, Wife, and Mother.*" And as Rosie grows older and is eventually presented, she'll also get those books on ballroom manners and fan flirting like the ones I used to have when I was in Lady Bradshaw's house.

And then I realize that even though I feel disdain toward the company Constance keeps, and the awfully boring conversations the ladies have when the men go hunting—it's inevitable that they can't talk much beyond gossip. They've been brought up to be ignorant and taught not to think for themselves. What else can they do when the resources aren't provided for them?

"Kat!"

Rosie has left her desk; she has her nose pressed against the window. "Thomas . . . he went rowing in the lake, and he's fallen in!"

I rush to the window. Outside, a small boat is bobbing on the lake while Thomas flails in the waters, one arm clawing the air.

"Doesn't he know how to swim?"

"No one taught him!" Rosie clutches my arm. "Oh, Kat, what can we do? Papa and Mama have gone to the village, and I don't even know who can swim."

I don't even pause to think. "I can."

❦

I RACE TOWARD THE LAKE AS FAST AS I CAN. ONCE I STOP AT the bank, I try to take off my gown but without success. My fingers fumble at the convoluted web of laces, and the more I try, the tighter I lace myself. Frustrated, I rip the laces off my dress. It falls on the ground in a heavy heap of velvet. Next I cast off my corset. Now with only my chemise on, I dive into the lake.

My heart contracts when the ice-cold water hits me. The sun may be shining, but it is still autumn. But I don't have time to think about it. I swim over to Thomas, who is still struggling in the water. I grab his arm, fully intending to drag him back to the bank, but then he fastens his arms around my neck in a death grip. We both go down in the water.

██████ If he doesn't loosen his hold on me, we could both drown. I open my mouth but swallow a mouthful of water. I can't tell him to let go. And even if I could, I very much doubt he would listen to me.

I struggle to get Thomas to loosen his grip, but he holds fast to me. He might only be thirteen, but his strength is already more than I can handle. For a moment, I apologize to Edward. *I'm sorry that I can't be with you for the remaining months.*

But then I hear Edward's voice in my head. *We still have nine months left. Make them the happiest nine months I have yet to live.*

A newfound strength rises within me. I manage to wrench my arm free from his grasp. But instead of trying to get Thomas back to shore, I punch him in the face—hard. That does the trick. He sags from the blow, falling limp in my arms.

I say a prayer of thanks, but my troubles aren't over yet. I'm not sure if I'm strong enough to drag him back to the shore. After a moment of hesitation, I start to head toward the boat. After much difficulty, I manage to dump him on it. I swim back to the bank, towing the boat with the unconscious boy on it.

"Kat!"

Rosie and several servants are now standing on the bank, their eyes as round as saucers. I deposit Thomas on the grass and check his pulse. He is still unconscious, so I tilt his head back and clamp my mouth over his, using what health class taught us about mouth-to-mouth resuscitation.

"What are you doing?" the steward cries.

"Trying to save his life," I snap.

I continue with the ministrations, ignoring the horrified looks on their faces. *Please wake up,* I pray frantically. *Please open your eyes.* A few minutes later, my prayers are answered. Thomas starts to gurgle and cough, and water dribbles down his chin. Then his eyes flicker open, and he looks up at me, his expression dazed.

I let out a huge sigh of relief. If he didn't wake up . . . if he didn't wake up . . .

A choked cry comes from Rosie.

A servant—the housekeeper, I think—gasps. "Praise the Lord—he's alive!"

I get to my feet—wet, cold, and shivering. But then a gust of wind comes up, and I sneeze.

"Can someone get me a towel?"

❧ 14 ❧

I sit in bed, propped up by two pillows, warming my hands with a mug of hot chocolate. I have a hot water bottle snuggled near my feet, and as if that isn't enough, thick blankets provide layers of comfort. A huge fire burns in the grate, with a servant bringing more logs. Another servant told me that the estate gets pretty cold during the winter, so they are well equipped for dealing with the cold.

I've just taken a hot bath, and my hair is still damp, wrapped in a towel. Wearing only my chemise, I wiggle my toes and drink some chocolate, enjoying the warmth that spreads from my stomach to my body.

"Where is she?" Edward's voice is urgent, commanding, as though if he's prevented from seeing me, he'll put everyone under arrest. The door is flung open, and he storms inside, ignoring the cries of, "But she is indecent!"

He sits on the bed, which sags from his weight. He searches my face, his gaze filled with concern. "Are you feeling well? Any injuries? Has the doctor been sent for?"

"Yes, no, and no. I'm feeling fine now that I'm out of the lake."

He still looks at me in disbelief, as though I said I just emerged unscathed from a building on fire. "I heard that you saved Thomas from drowning. How did you survive the waters? The lake is much deeper than the river at the Fremont house."

"Oh. I'm . . . we had swimming lessons in high school," I say in a low voice. "And my father took me to the pool when I was a kid. I know it sounds impossible, but yeah, it's not uncommon for a girl to know how to swim where I come from."

He lets out a sigh and pushes his hair from his face. "I should have known. When they told me you dived into the lake, I . . ." He swallows and looks away. "I thought it was only by a stroke of luck, or because help arrived just in time, that you survived."

I put my hand on his. "I'm sorry," I whisper, "but there wasn't anyone nearby. I couldn't let him drown."

"No." He threads his fingers through mine and tightens his grip. "That is not what you should apologize for."

Instantly, I know what he is referring to. My stomach tightens, and I look down at our hands clasped together. "Krev visited me."

"The goblin you have mentioned? The one who is responsible for sending you here?"

I nod. In a low voice, I repeat what Krev told me about my changing Athelia's history—and about the old Katriona coming back.

"I'm sorry," I say again, "but I'm scared—worried for you. I'd hate it if you were stuck with someone you didn't know. What if she is as horrible as Bianca?"

When I look up, my heart jumps. His face is so close that his breath warms my cheeks. His eyes are blazing; my instinct is to back away, but the headboard prevents me putting any distance between us.

"Even if that happens"—his voice is low but underlaid with passion—"it is *my* choice. I'll handle whatever comes after you're gone. But *now*, all I want is to make the most of my time with you, and yet you choose to foist another girl on me. Did you ever consider how I might feel? Have you forgotten what I told you that day?"

The anguish in his voice is palpable. Remorse, shame, and affection for him rise up within me; a lump forms in my throat, and tears start to gather in my eyes.

"I'm sorry," I say again, blinking away the tears. "I shouldn't have tried . . . it was thoughtless of me."

His expression softens, though the sternness in his eyes is still there. Footsteps approach the door; he looks back for a second but ignores whoever is coming our way.

"I should teach you a lesson for your heartlessness, Kat." He says it with such a serious face that for a second I wonder if he's joking.

"Are you saying that what I did warrants a punishment?"

"Correct."

His hands clamp down on the blankets around my hips. Edward leans in and kisses me, completely disregarding the open door, completely ignoring the fact that I am only wearing a chemise, completely forgetting that he shouldn't be initiating such intimacy before marriage. Nevertheless, I don't bother to dissuade him. I bunch my fingers on the hem of his coat and pour my feelings into the kiss—partly to make up for the pain I'll cause when I leave, but mostly for encouraging him to warm up to Lillie.

Someone coughs loudly. Edward breaks off the kiss and stands up, and I catch a flash of annoyance in his eyes. There, in the doorway, stand Philip, Constance, and a bunch of other lords and ladies, all of them wearing identical expressions of pure shock. Lady Fremont has a hand over her mouth. There's also Lillie, who looks like someone struck her on the head. She meets my eyes for a second and suddenly dashes off. I can almost hear her heart breaking.

Well, there goes any hope of finding a substitute for Edward when I'm gone. But now I don't feel any remorse. I promised Edward that we'd be the happiest couple in Athelia, and this time, I swear I will keep my promise.

"Well, although I am glad that Katriona is well," Philip says, a grin tugging at the corners of his mouth, "might I remind you, my dear cousin, that you are not married yet. Even though I can perfectly comprehend your feelings."

"Not to mention that you aren't even officially engaged," Constance says. Her tone is more severe—not surprising, since she's a stickler for propriety.

I sneeze just at that moment. Edward reaches into his pocket and gives me his handkerchief. "Send for the doctor immediately. I will not have Kat develop a cold."

❧

OUR REMAINING FEW DAYS AT NORTHPORT ARE THE HAPPIEST I have experienced since entering the palace. I caught a cold after all—not surprising, considering that I was standing for a while before a servant brought me a towel—and was ordered to stay in bed until His Royal Fussiness and the physician decided I was well enough to leave. It's almost like being Jane Bennet, although however attentive Edward behaves, his manner will always seem more Darcy-ish to me.

Edward seems smugly content—which I soon discover why. After that public demonstration that borders on scandalous, my reputation is as good as ruined by my would-be fiancé. It also sent a message to the others: the prince was so overcome with relief that his beloved is safe that he couldn't control himself in an irrational display of passion. It will be an ill-considered move to separate us.

I'm both embarrassed and pleased. To think that the best way to safeguard from being tricked into a compromising position is to simply engage in the compromising position ourselves.

"Are you sure it's okay if you don't go out with them?" I ask. Duke Philip and the men have just left for another grouse-shooting expedition in the moors. From the bed, I can see them astride their horses, the brass holsters of the guns poking from their hips.

Edward settles on a stool by the bed. "Perfectly sure. In fact, I have to thank you. This is the perfect excuse I need to not join the hunt. I always prefer to create a life rather than to extinguish one."

There's a rustle of skirts. Constance enters, followed by an array of servants. She waves a hand like a commander, and they go to work like well-trained soldiers. One stokes the fireplace, another clears the dishes on my breakfast tray, and yet another changes the hot water bottle.

"My dear Katriona! Do tell me that you are feeling better this morning. We were *so* concerned about you, and your presence at breakfast was sorely missed."

"Um . . ." Considering that I rarely speak more than a sentence or two among them, I suppose she's just being polite, especially since Edward's also there. "I'm sorry. Actually, I'm almost recovered. I would have attended breakfast if *someone*"— I send Edward a meaningful look—"hadn't insisted on treating me like a porcelain doll."

"It is for the safety of others, as well," Edward says with his emotionless face on. "To prevent them from being infected from your cold."

I roll my eyes. "And you are immune?"

He doesn't even blink. "Henry has always told me my constitution is as impregnable as a fortress."

Constance looks between us, her beautiful brown eyes blinking. "Now, now—let us not have a tiff in the morning. Honestly, my dear"—she looks at me and shakes a slender finger that would look perfect on a piano—"you ought be more appreciative of such affection, not to mention that he is the prince. And you, young man, must be prepared to endure grudges and grumbling from the menfolk."

Edward raises an eyebrow. He looks genuinely puzzled. "Why?"

"At breakfast, all the ladies could talk of nothing but how you refused to leave Katriona's side. Now all the husbands will be nagged about how they should aspire to your level of attentiveness."

I giggle. Edward chooses to turn to the window in dignified silence, but a telltale blush is spreading from his neck to his ears. I'm tempted to tease him, but I decide not to since Constance is still here.

"How is Thomas, by the way?"

Constance nods. "Lords bless him; he is doing all right. We gave him a right good scolding, and he's forbidden to go out for the entire week."

"Teach him how to swim," Edward says, his tone frigid. "As well as Tristan and Liana."

"*Rosie*? But—"

"Unless you prefer that she never walk near the lake or go rowing?"

Constance looks scandalized. "You cannot suggest that my only daughter, brought up with propriety and care, go *swimming* in the open air. Have you not considered her reputation? What will the neighbors think?"

"It is, of course, not my place to advise how you raise your children. Remember, however, that were Kat not present when Thomas fell in, he might have drowned."

"Pardon me," I add, straightening my spine. "But having talked to Rosie, I do believe that she wishes to learn more than simply the lessons you have assigned her." I give an account of how Thomas bullied Rosie and how she preferred to work on math problems than her needlework. "I'm not saying that her . . . um . . . lady lessons are bad, but should we not respect her desire to broaden her knowledge?"

Constance purses her lips; obviously she's conflicted between the conventional way of raising her daughter and the new information that I have presented. "But even if I allow Rosie to take different lessons, there are no resources. The governess knows very little other than literature and music. And it's impossible that I send her to boarding school along with Tristan and Thomas."

I fold my hands and give her my best imperial gaze, perfected by practice with Madame Dubois. "That you need not be worried about. I am already involved in the planning for a girls' school. Both rich and poor will be allowed to attend, so girls can receive a practical education—not a superficial one that revolves around pleasing menfolk. Will you allow Rosie to be sent to the school when it opens?"

A brief look of surprise from Edward, but his reaction is just beautiful. "You may be assured that this girls' school will receive full support from the crown."

Silence ensues. "But . . . I don't . . ." It's the first time I've seen Constance stammer. "I must have time to think it over."

"Certainly." I smile at her encouragingly. "I look forward to a favorable reply."

When Constance leaves us, Edward comes to my side and threads his fingers through mine. I look into his eyes, and my heart feels like bursting from the admiring, affectionate gaze in his face. It has been some time since he looked at me like that. "Now *that* is the Kat I know and love."

❧ 15 ❧

Edward slips the engagement ring onto my finger. It is set with emeralds, diamonds, white topaz, amethysts, and rubies—gemstones that form his name. Somehow, the jeweler was able to fashion the gems in a pattern that doesn't look too flashy, for which I'm thankful.

It's the day that our engagement is officially announced. Edward and I stand in the center of a room, surrounded by close friends and relatives. They will witness the ceremony of the man presenting his engagement gift, which is typically a ring.

The king and queen wear simple but elegant crimson robes, both of them smiling broadly. Mr. Davenport has his arm around Poppy, who isn't showing, but she has a hand over her stomach already. Elle stands near them, looking fresh and lovely in a pale, pink gown. I might have imagined it, but I catch her glance at Henry across the room and a smile, small but sweet, blossoms in her face. Edward told me that Henry, much to the duchess's displeasure, offered to give biology lectures in the new girls' school. Score one for Henry. This definitely means he is making progress in his relationship with Elle.

Lady Bradshaw, my "mother" in Story World, wears an uncertain, awkward smile. I think she still hasn't gotten over the shock that it is I who caught the prince's eye, not her other movie-star-gorgeous daughter. Out of the corner of my eye, I glimpse Bianca—tall and regal and her lips formed in a tight smile. She disappeared when Duke Philip invited us to his mansion. Later, Meg informed me that my "sister" tried to seek the fairies, possibly in the hopes of getting a spell di amor, or something similar, to ensnare the prince. She was unsuccessful in her quest as few people actually knew where the fae resided. After days of searching in vain, she returned and resigned herself to an offer from Lord Mansfield's nephew.

"This is heavier than I expected." I hold up my hand; the jewels gleam in the light. "I won't be able to hold a fan during future balls."

"That won't be necessary." Edward smirks. "Your inability to command grace and elegance eliminates the need to carry a fan."

I raise my eyebrows in mock anger. "How dare you insult me so! I suppose I shall have to withhold the gift I prepared for you."

Now it's his turn to raise his eyebrows, though it's an expression of pure surprise. "A gift? For me?"

I signal to Amelie, who comes forward with a small, dark blue box wrapped in white ribbons. Edward opens the box and lifts out a silver watch chain with a heart-shaped fob attached to it. I motion for him to flip the fob over. Engraved on the back are our initials in long, loopy letters, entwined in an embrace.

Edward looks up, his gaze filled with affection. I swear, if there weren't others present, he would kiss me on the spot.

"How did you acquire this?"

"Stole it when the shopkeeper wasn't looking." Nearby, the duchess deals me a glare. I smile and wink at her. "Well, actually

. . . I bought it from the proceeds of my interview of the children. Mr. Wellesley wrote me a check."

Edward smiles. "And you chose to spend it on me." Carefully, he fastens his pocket watch to the chain and puts it in his pocket. Then he takes my hand. "Now, I daresay it is time that we face the public."

Outside, reporters are gathered in the courtyard. A flash goes off, making me feel as though I'm in Hollywood. I was amazed when the king and queen told me that there would be a press conference after the gift ceremony, but if the papers can print my story on child labor, they can certainly cover a report on the royal engagement.

Edward leads me to the top of a flight of stairs that leads down to the courtyard. Bertram and several other palace guards stand at the foot of the stairs to prevent any unruly person from getting too close.

My palms start to sweat. I've rarely had any experience in public speaking—apart from that one-time outburst in the park, when I was so incensed by a stranger doubting my report on child labor. But this is different. I am now princess of Athelia and have to maintain a dignified presence in public.

"Your Highness!" a bushy-haired reporter yells. "I wager a hundred people have already asked you this question, but our readers really want to know—of all the girls in the ball, what made you choose Lady Katriona Bradshaw?"

Edward grins. "Believe it or not, I had been courting her before the ball. It took me a long time, but eventually she accepted my proposal."

Murmurs of disbelief run through the crowd. A few people look at each other and shrug—obviously this was *not* the answer they were expecting.

"Er . . . Lady Katriona," the same reporter asks. "Can you tell us the reason for your hesitation?" He doesn't say it, but he could have added, *Normally any girl would be delighted to have the prince.*

"I was an idiot."

More noises from the crowd. Yeah, that was definitely not the answer they expected, either.

"But now that I've come to my senses"—I squeeze Edward's hand—"I pledge you, Prince Edward of Athelia, my undivided devotion and eternal affection. Forever."

THE END

READ ON FOR AN EXCERPT FROM THE SEQUEL, *TWICE UPON a Time*—>

TWICE UPON A TIME TEASER

Book Description: Seven years have passed since Kat left Athelia. Through the intervention of the goblin king's baby daughter, the book is re-opened and Kat is transported back to Story World. Upon learning she is given a second chance, Edward is determined not to let her go this time. His chance of succeeding, however, seems like nil. Kat doesn't remember anything of their past, she loathes life at court, and she's anxious to return to modern world. Not to mention that there's a price to pay for tampering with the book again...

"And they lived happily ever after."

A happy sigh rose from the baby goblin girl. She was sprawled on the floor, face upturned, her large, yellow, cat-like eyes shining with joy. Next to her sat a middle-aged goblin wearing spectacles with a book propped on his legs, the binding creased and the pages worn. Except for the sparkling golden crown sitting askew on his head, he looked rather ordinary.

"How many children did they have, Daddy?"

"The book doesn't tell us, sweetie. It just ends with their wedding."

"But what about Kat's family in her human world? Did she ever see them again?"

"Of course she did. She returned to the human world once she completed her mission."

The child gave a horrified gasp. "So, she just *left* Edward standing at the altar like that?"

"He wasn't left alone, pumpkin. The original Katriona returned to her body, so he still has a bride. Edward arranged it so that no one would suspect Kat had switched places with the storybook Katriona. And Kat remembers nothing about her life in the fairy tale, so she is spared the pain of losing her true love. Don't worry your pretty little head about it."

Said pretty little head was now shaking in pure outrage. "That's not a happy ending, Daddy! You lied to me! You lied!"

"Pippi!" The goblin king exclaimed. "Do stop bawling, angel."

"You're such a meanie! I'm never trusting you again!"

Barthelius tried to calm her down by ruffling her hair, but his fingers grew tangled in her mountain of extraordinarily curly hair—hair that reminded him of that corkscrew-shaped pasta humans called fusilli. "Really, there's no need to be so distressed about the ending. Let's read another story together, shall we? Or do you want to see the new doll Daddy got for you?"

He looked around at his court, silently pleading for one of them to offer a helping hand. Unfortunately for him, it was the goblins' nature to take pleasure in another's misfortune. Most of them only shrugged innocently or tried to mask their grins behind knobby hands.

Barthelius had no choice but to exert his absolute power as king.

"Krev!" he barked. A long-suffering goblin slunk slowly to his side. He had a face that looked as though he were squashed and ironed as a baby. "Take the princess down to the nursery.

Give her another book or toy or candy—it doesn't matter. When I come back, I want to see her pacified."

Krev looked alarmed at the prospect of calming the little princess. "But Your Majesty . . ."

"It's all your fault," Barthelius muttered. "You should have united the real Cinderella together with the prince, instead of letting Katherine Wilson continue to interact with him."

"Who, me?" Krev raised one thick, worm-like eyebrow. "Your Majesty was the one most amused when the plot went awry. We were taking bets every time I had a new report to make. Why, the queen even won a purse of gold!"

"That was before I could anticipate *this*—" Barthelius jerked his thumb at the spectacle on the floor beside him. His daughter was now rolling across the floor, her wails filling the air. "I had no idea she would be so fixated on that damn book. It's been how many—six years?"

"Seven."

"Hmph. It seems like only yesterday that we witnessed the completion of that book."

"Can't we rip up *The Ugly Stepsister* instead?"

Barthelius raised his eyebrows and jabbed a finger at Krev's chest. "To borrow a human phrase: You. Are. Nuts. First, how are you going to track down Katherine Wilson after so many years? Second, how is she going to tear up the book when it's only seven years old? You can't compel a human to act unless through forbidden magic. You know the rules. Third, let's assume she re-entered the book. The prince is already married to the real Katriona Bradshaw—are you asking him to divorce his wife and marry the human? Even if he risks the wrath of the entire kingdom by leaving a wife who did him no wrong, Katherine Wilson will *still* have to return to the human world once she has completed the happy ending! You're going to break the prince's heart twice."

Krev heaved a sigh. His ears and shoulders drooped. "Come

along, Your Highness," he called to the little goblin princess. "Want to hear a secret story of Kat and Edward—one that didn't appear in the book?"

Pippi asked so many questions that Krev suspected that were she living in the human world, she'd be one of those diehard fans who created book trailers and wrote fanfiction and dressed up as characters in the story. He pictured her wearing a ball gown and acting out a court presentation to the queen . . . no. The dumpy figure of a typical goblin was simply unsuited for huge frilly dresses. They usually wore plain, sack-like clothes. Goblins weren't known for their fashion sense.

"Why is your face all scrunched up, Krev?" Pippi asked, her eyes alight with curiosity. "You look like you've swallowed a lemon."

Like a child being caught stealing from a jar of cookies, Krev tried to look innocent instead. Most goblins would have declared him a poor actor, but fortunately, the little princess wasn't that perceptive. Yet. "Nothing, Your Highness."

Pippi hugged the book close to her chest. Of all the books Barthelius had created, it was this messed-up version of *Cinderella* that she enjoyed most. She belonged to the post-office—or wait, was it post-modern?—category of readers who preferred their heroines strong and feisty. The damsel-in-distress was a thing of the past.

"Did you actually see Kat return to her family?"

Krev scratched his head. A couple of long, mottled-green hairs fell off. Dang, his premature baldness was speeding to the finish line.

"Did you?"

"Well . . . yes. There wasn't anything we could do about it. The spell works automatically. Once she fulfilled the happily-ever-after requirement, she was compelled to leave. She had no choice but to return to her mother and sister in the human world."

"But why couldn't she go back for a while to say goodbye, and then come back? Oh, the poor prince! You can't leave him stuck with a girl he doesn't love!"

Krev heaved yet another sigh. He lost count of how many times he'd sighed when talking to Pippi. Really, it was entirely Barthelius and Morag's fault for spoiling her and giving her whatever she wanted when she wanted it. Every toy she demanded had to be given to her, and every candy she coveted had to be procured. "Once the book is completed, it stays that way forever. It's permanent."

Pippi banged on the table with a fist. A crack appeared on the surface. Krev made a private note to mention to the king that the princess's strength was showing early. "You've got to get them back together! It's so UNFAIR to keep them apart!"

"Your Highness, unfortunately, the spell doesn't work that way—"

"I don't care! I want a happy ending for Kat and Edward! I want it NOOOOOOOW!"

Pippi stalked to her room, sniffling. Everyone was useless. Why were they all okay about Edward and Kat being apart? How could they be so heartless? Didn't they all tell her that fairy tales end with happily-ever-after?

"Liars," she muttered, scuffing her small foot on the ground. "Why didn't Daddy stop Kat from returning to America? I don't want Edward to marry another girl—he and Kat were perfect for each other! And how could Kat agree to leave him? Why couldn't she remember him anymore? Did somebody put a spell on her?"

"Your mother did."

Pippi whirled around so fast that her short legs got tangled into each other and she landed on the floor with an undignified bump. "Who—who are you?"

Another goblin, who seemed around her father's age, hovered above her, his wings flapping. He looked friendly, but Pippi wasn't sure that she liked his crooked grin.

"Morag put a strong memory charm on the human being because she knew the girl could become seriously depressed if she went home with the prince on her mind. It was hard enough that she had to choose between her family and him."

"But what about Edward? Did Mommy also make him forget Kat?"

The goblin wagged a finger at her. "Morag offered, but he refused. The real Katriona would return to her body once the human girl's soul left, and he needed his memory intact to deal with her. Besides, he didn't want to forget Katherine Wilson."

Pippi promptly burst into tears. "That's so cruel!" she wailed. "Kat should be the one with him, not the other girl!"

"That can be accomplished."

The wailing stopped. Pippi stared at the goblin with huge, suspicious eyes.

"What did you say?"

The goblin tilted his chin upward. "I am Borg the Invincible, elder brother of Barthelius. Your father was afraid of my powers, and he feared that I'd overpower him and take his throne one day, so he devised a plan and stole most of my magic away."

Pippi gasped. "Daddy wouldn't do that! He always said it's wrong to steal."

"He told you that you shouldn't steal, but did he say it's wrong for him? Parents." Borg sneered. "Always nagging at the kids while failing to set a good example themselves. Anyway, do you or do you not want to see the human girl reunited with the Athelian prince?"

"Of course!" Pippi jumped up. "Can you really do that, Uncle Borg?"

Borg's eyes gleamed. "With enough magic, it shall be no problem. However, Barthelius would never agree to perform the spell, so it will depend on you."

Pippi didn't understand. What did this have to do with her? She was only five. She didn't know how to cast any spells. Barthelius and Morag refused to teach her until she was at least a few years older and had a better grasp on her magic.

"Barthelius doesn't want to see me," Borg said. "He knows I've been trying to get my magic back, so he will try to banish me from court as soon as he lays eyes on me. But you, the daughter of the king, can get it."

"You want me to steal?"

"It isn't called stealing, sweetie, just returning an object to its rightful owner."

Pippi frowned. "If there was a spell that could send Kat back to Edward, why didn't Daddy tell me about it?"

"Because it's forbi—because your father isn't confident in his abilities to wield so much magic. It takes a truly powerful spell to send a human girl from one realm to another. And if you want Katherine Wilson to return before the prince is married, you will need to perform a time reversal spell as well. All this together will cost big magic—enormous magic, I tell you."

Pippi chewed on her lip. The book, still tightly grasped in her arms, seemed to grow warmer. What would Daddy say if he found out? He'd be mad, for sure, but if he did steal from Uncle Borg in the first place . . .

"How am I going to get the magic?"

"Easy. It's sealed in that emerald green ring your father has on his forefinger. Get it and bring it to me. I'll regain my magic in an instant."

"How do I know you are telling the truth?"

"Suspicious little thing, aren't you?" Borg held up his hands. He had short, stubby fingers—quite a contrast to Barthelius's long, slender ones. "Suppose we do a simple pact that won't need much magic? Repeat after me: I, Princess Pippi, daughter of King Barthelius, will retrieve the emerald ring for Borg the Invincible. In return for your efforts, I, Borg the Invincible, swear to transport Katherine Wilson to Athelia, and also to revert Athelia to the exact moment when Prince Edward's wedding takes place, in order for Katherine Wilson to resume her relationship with him without further complications. There, are you satisfied?"

Pippi hesitated. Yellow-green light glowed from Borg's hands. Then, with a determined nod, she held out her chubby little hands, and the light twisted and wove around their hands like a pair of serpents.

Click *HERE* to get the full book *Twice Upon A Time*!

AFTERWORD

It's not over yet! Kat will meet Edward again in Book 2, *Twice Upon a Time*.

Would you like to learn about my future projects (more fairy tale retellings & fantasy)? Sign up for my newsletter! http://www.ayaling.com/newsletter.html

What you'll get for joining the club:

1. Receive an exclusive short story told from Edward's point of view, plus extra/deleted scenes. I may add new material from time to time once I get the ideas.

2. Be the first to know when I have a new release.

3. Be the first to know when I give away free stuff, call for advanced readers, run a poll, or other fun activities.

See you next book!

-Aya-

BOOKS BY AYA

UNFINISHED FAIRY TALES

The Ugly Stepsister (Book 1)

Princess of Athelia (Book 1.5)

Twice Upon a Time (Book 2)

Ever After (Book 3)

Queen of Athelia (Book 4)

THE PRINCESS SERIES

Princesses Don't Get Fat

Princesses Don't Fight in Skirts

Princesses Don't Become Engineers

GIRL WITH FLYING WEAPONS

Girl with Flying Weapons

ABOUT THE AUTHOR

Aya is from Taiwan, where she struggles daily to contain her obsession with mouthwatering and unhealthy foods. Often she will devour a good book instead. Her favourite books include martial arts romances, fairy tale retellings, high fantasy, cozy mysteries, and manga.

www.ayaling.com

 facebook.com/ayalingwriter

 twitter.com/ayalingling

Made in the USA
Middletown, DE
24 December 2018